ACCORDING TO AUDREY

To Oona.

HAPPY LaShelle

Praise & Confidence!

Happy
LaShelle

ACCORDING TO AUDREY
Copyright ©2018 Happy LaShelle
All rights reserved.
Printed in the United States of America
First Edition: May 2018

WWW.CLEANTEENPUBLISHING.COM

Summary: Cautious and introverted, seventeen-year-old Dove spends most of her free time pursuing her one true love: painting. Her favorite subjects are the stuff of Audrey Hepburn films as she daydreams about romance. A hotshot jock is exactly not the type of guy she's been looking for—but when Leo Donovan drops his cool act to show his vulnerable side, Dove begins to question everything...

ISBN: 978-1-63422-276-1 (paperback)
ISBN: 978-1-63422-277-8 (e-book)
Cover Design by: Marya Heidel
Typography by: Courtney Knight
Editing by: Cynthia Shepp

COVER ART
© DAVIDARTS / FOTOLIA
© MELANJURGA / FOTOLIA

Young Adult Fiction / Coming of Age
Young Adult Fiction / Social Themes / Dating & Sex
Young Adult Fiction / Girls & Women
Young Adult Fiction / Media Tie-In

For more information about our content disclosure, please utilize the QR code above with your smart phone or visit us at WWW.CLEANTEENPUBLISHING.COM.

For Havilyn,
who reminded me to write

Chapter 1

My feet dangled off the edge of the boat dock. Gentle waves lapped against the weathered wood, revealing the mussels and green moss clinging to its side. The harbor was quiet. Only a small whaler chugged along, cutting through the gray-blue water, leaving tiny whitecaps in its wake. This was my favorite time of day, early evening, when the last rays of sunlight glistened on the bay. As long as I could remember, I'd watched the sunset over this dock.

I dipped my brush into the palette of paint and water beside me and touched it to the pad of pressed paper in my lap. My hand glided over the page, guiding the smooth, pointed tip, and a soft shade of blue skimmed onto the paper. From the paint to the page, I skipped the brush back and forth, the image of the bay slowly taking shape.

Only a few strokes into capturing the outline of a tethered sailboat, my phone buzzed inside my pocket.

Text message.

Need you! Get over here now!

I hopped up and grabbed my paint supplies, placing them into the large storage chest on the dock's edge and then headed toward the house, phone in hand. The wood planks creaked under my bare feet as I quickly typed.

What's wrong?

Once upstairs, I pulled my blue sweater over my head, slipped on my black ballet flats, and high-fived my *Breakfast at Tiffany's* poster the way I always did before I flicked off the light.

For me, it was the same concept as a football player slapping the team logo when heading out of the locker room and into the stadium. Tapping Audrey's smiling face every time I left my bedroom made me feel like, somehow, I was tapping into her essence. Because the one and only Audrey Hepburn was pretty much the definition of amazing.

Downstairs, the back of my stepbrother's blond head peeked out over the couch in the family room. He sat transfixed, headset attached and controller in hand, while he blasted away at some sort of Xbox creature. It had to be the ideal way for a ten-year-old boy to spend his Friday night. I messed his hair. "Griffin?"

"Yeah?" he answered, not turning his head.

"If anyone asks, tell them I went to Jessie's, okay?" I checked my phone for Jessie's response. Nothing.

He continued to stare at the screen, his thumbs flying over the buttons on the controller. "Mmkay."

Whether or not my message would be relayed was questionable, but I stepped out onto the front porch and shut the door behind me.

Jessie and I had always thought that living only a

few blocks away from each other was a huge stroke of luck. But the fact that we'd been best friends since first grade was something pretty special. Now, high school meant being surrounded by legions of Newport Beach girls, with the line often blurring between friends and enemies.

Heading down the steps, I checked my phone again just as Jessie's new text buzzed in, glaring back at me.

Sixth grade crush is here!

I stopped in my tracks, still staring down at my phone. Seriously? That was the big deal? Mark Mason, Jessie's middle school obsession, was the reason why I'd ditched such a gorgeous sunset? I looked over my shoulder as I contemplated going back to the dock, but the last bits of orange and pink lingering in the sky had almost disappeared. Too late. Slowly, I started toward Jessie's again, remembering how she used to drive me crazy with Mark Mason this and Mark Mason that. What was Mark doing over there, anyway?

Three blocks later I rounded the corner to the familiar sight of Jessie's white, two-story house with the red front door. I caught a glimpse of the big sycamore beyond the fence and let my gaze linger on the tree house in its branches. In the course of our lives, Jessie and I had spent about a thousand afternoons up in that tree.

I knocked on the front door and waited. No answer. Trying the doorbell would be useless... it had been broken for years. I grabbed the door handle and turned it. Locked. The faint beat of music drifted from somewhere inside, and I knocked again, louder this time. "Jess?" I called, and then looked over my shoulder at the path of large stepping-stones leading to the side gate.

The instant I turned toward the pathway, the front door flew open.

A guy with dark hair stood in the doorway, staring. I froze. His cheeks dimpled as he smiled at me, and his eyes glinted with recognition. He ran his fingers through his hair, pushing it backwards.

Oh. I blinked, finally understanding. *My sixth-grade crush.* I shifted my weight and tried to casually take in the sight of Leo Donovan.

"Hey, Dove." My name rolled out of his mouth as easygoing as ever.

"Hey, Leo." I tried to smile. "What are you, uh… doing in Newport?" I winced inside at how stupid I sounded.

He shrugged. "Just visiting my dad."

I gave him a polite nod and pushed my way past him into the house. *Figures he'd be answering someone else's door.* Apparently, he was just as full of himself as ever. Honestly, what my twelve-year-old self had seen in him I didn't know. Well… that wasn't exactly true. Twelve-year-old Dove had been rather impressed by his deep gaze and charming dimples. But seventeen-year-old Dove wasn't so easily blindsided—his middle school escapades had been enough for me to completely peg him as a player.

I scanned the family room, eager to find Jessie. A handful of kids hung out on the couches around the coffee table. Jessie's debate team buddy, Kai, was wedged on the sofa beside her boyfriend, Clive. Across from them sat a couple of other guys—including Isaiah, Jessie's on-again, off-again boyfriend. Right now, they were off again.

"Dovey!" Jessie called out. Her chestnut ponytail bounced back and forth as she rounded the corner from the hallway, picking up her pace toward me. "Dove's here!" she announced to the group.

"Hi." Kai smiled. Clive flicked his head back in a friendly way, as if to say 'hey' without actually saying it. The two of them had been together since freshman year, and not once had they broken up. Somehow, I could never come to a clear conclusion about it. Did their connection have to do with comfort, or was it something worth envying—like fate or destiny?

Jessie eyed Leo, then snapped her gaze back to me and stifled a smile. Resisting the urge to roll my eyes, I faked a carefree smile and made my way toward her.

In his oh-so-smooth way, Leo walked across the room, sat down on the coffee table, and bent over his cell phone.

I grabbed Jessie's arm. "Can you come here for a sec?" The loud music swallowed up my forced casual tone as I guided Jessie down the hallway and into the bathroom. Flipping on the light, I shut the door behind us and turned toward her. "Jess!" I snapped. "I stopped painting to rush over here."

Her face fell. "Oh, really? I'm sorry!"

I dipped my head sideways. It was impossible to stay mad at Jessie. "It's okay. I just thought this piece might be the one I'd enter in the fair."

"I thought you were entering the one you did of the Balboa Ferry..."

"I don't know if it's good enough. I can't decide." I let out a breath.

The Orange County Fair had rolled around yet again, and Saturday was entry day. This year I really needed to win. A Parsons Paris scholarship was not an easy one to earn, and if I were somehow going to get to Europe next fall, it wouldn't be through the good graces of my dad and stepmom.

Patty had made it perfectly clear that Europe wasn't an option. According to her not-so-humble opinion, the cost and safety issues made the whole idea ridiculous. And as far as my dad was concerned, the only art school to consider was The Art Institute of Chicago because Chi-town was his hometown—the best city in the world. And why would anyone want to go anywhere else?

No, if there was any possibility of making Paris happen, it was up to me to figure out a way. If I could organize it all and pay for it myself, then how could they possibly say no? Unfortunately, my hours working at the art gallery wouldn't begin to make a dent in the cost of Parsons' tuition. A merit scholarship was the only way—and a Best of Show ribbon in one of the state's biggest fairs could give me the edge I needed.

Jessie bit her lip. "I really am sorry. I was so surprised when Leo showed up with Isaiah, and I just thought maybe you'd want to see him... you know, see what he looks like now and all." Jessie raised her eyebrows as though what he looked like was definitely worth seeing.

I couldn't stop my smile. "Okay, whatever, he's pretty hot. The problem is, he knows it. Let's face it, the guy who won the make-out contest with Lindsay Clifford on the blacktop in middle school is destined to be a complete jerk in high school."

Jessie snorted a laugh. "I forgot about that."

"Yeah, well, I didn't." It was surprising how much the memory stung. I straightened my shoulders. "Besides, he wasn't my first crush, my first crush was—"

"If you say Humphrey Bogart I'm gonna kill you."

"But Humphrey *was* my first crush!"

"Okay, stubborn one—we're talking about reality here, not your Audrey Hepburn delusions." Jessie rolled

6

her eyes. "Seriously, don't try to pretend you weren't head over heels for Leo."

"I wasn't!" A warm tingle crept into my cheeks. "And even if I *was*—"

"Aha!" Jessie cried, grinning triumphantly.

"—Then that was about a bazillion years ago."

"More like six." Jessie laughed.

"Six..." The number stopped me. Six years. I met Jessie's gaze, and her smirk slowly faded to a frown as I swallowed hard, slowing down. "Next month."

I had been so caught up with the art show lately, I hadn't even thought about the fact that September was just around the corner. And September always brought with it one dark reminder: the fact that another year had passed with my mom gone. Forever. Tears welled, but I bit the inside of my cheek to hold them back.

"Oh, Dovey." Jessie wrapped her arms around me without saying another word. After all, what was left to say? Every sympathetic word had been spoken. Endless tears had been cried. All the horrific anguish had been agonized over, time and again. So why didn't this hellish anniversary ever get any easier? Cancer had stolen my mom away, and with her, some special part of me seemed to have vanished, too.

I brushed away the few tears that had escaped and squeezed Jessie hard. "Thanks, Jess." I took a deep breath, gathering myself.

Jessie smoothed my hair as she stepped back.

I exhaled. "I'm just... really worried about the show. *Piper* is entering."

Jessie shrugged. "You always beat her."

"Except for last year." I fixed my gaze on my reflection in the mirror beside Jessie and stared into my own eyes as if to challenge myself. Losing to Piper was *not* an option, and no matter what Jessie said, Piper was definitely tough competition.

Jessie eyed me sideways. "Well, you'd better stay now. It would be super weird if you just left and went home. We'll order pizza or something and then you can leave."

"Fine." I breathed a tiny groan. "I'll stay for pizza."

The loud beat of the music floated toward us again as we entered the family room, side by side. Out of the corner of my eye, I checked out Leo's reaction. He was still absorbed in whatever it was on his phone. Texting a girl, no doubt.

"Should we get some pizza?" Jessie flopped into an oversized chair next to the couch.

I glanced around. The only place left to sit was on the coffee table next to Leo, and that was not about to happen. I squared my shoulders and crossed my arms, counting the minutes until dinner would be over and I could get back to work. Now that my last-ditch effort for a painting of the sunset was no longer an option, I'd have to put the finishing touches on a different one. Was the painting of the ferry good enough? The background needed fixing. More yellow maybe.

"Let's order from Gina's." Isaiah's statement snapped me back to the moment.

"They don't deliver," Leo said without looking up from his phone. I wasn't sure what annoyed me more—his know-it-all attitude about Newport Beach, or the fact that he'd made himself so at home in Jessie's living room.

"That's okay, we can pick it up," Jessie said, grabbing a piece of paper from the coffee table. "What do we want?"

Clive and a few of the guys called out toppings.

"Want anything, Leo?" Isaiah asked.

Leo lifted his head and his hair fell into his eyes. "I'll just have whatever you guys are ordering."

"Who are you texting?" Isaiah sounded amused.

Leo shrugged. "No one. I'm checking the Angels score."

I let my brow wrinkle just a little. I wouldn't have pegged him for a baseball kind of guy.

"Who's coming with?" Jessie picked up her keys.

"Me," I answered without hesitating. There was no way I was going to stay there and hang out with Isaiah and his posse.

Jessie turned to Kai. "Wanna come, too?"

Kai's head rested against Clive's shoulder, and her arms were wrapped around his waist. "Okay," she said, like she wasn't really sure, but she still managed to pull herself away from him. I forced myself to look away. For a girl who was president of the debate team, Kai sure didn't seem to voice any kind of opinion when she was in Clive's vicinity.

Clive flicked his head again, this time at Jessie. "I'm gonna tell some more people to come over. Everyone wanted to know what was up tonight..."

"No, don't," Jessie interrupted. "My mom said only a few people." She turned to Isaiah, who was now lying on the couch. "And *you* had better get your feet off there. These sofas are brand new. If anything happens to them, she'll freak out."

JESSIE'S JEEP SPED ACROSS the bay bridge, passing the Back Bay along Pacific Coast Highway to Corona Del Mar. As we neared Gina's Pizza, I glanced over at the familiar front of the Port Theater and drew in a slow breath. My mom and I had spent about a hundred weekend afternoons inside those tall, glass doors. Anything featuring old Hollywood stars would do, but when an Audrey Hepburn film played we always showed up early and waited at the ready for the opening credits with buckets of popcorn in our laps.

In one of the windows, a black-and-white vintage Hollywood movie poster advertised the weekly Sunday matinee. I squinted to read it but caught only a glimpse of a couple embracing. Was that *Roman Holiday*? I made a mental note to check on it later. Missing Audrey on the big screen would be unforgivable.

WE WALKED OUT OF Gina's with our arms full of take-out boxes, and I hoisted myself into the back seat, helping to pile the warm pizzas beside me. The top was off the Jeep for the summer, and as we sped home, my hair whipped around in the cool air.

"So, how long is Leo in town?" Jessie's question to Kai caught my attention, and I didn't miss her playful smile in the rearview mirror.

"He's here visiting his dad for the summer," Kai answered. "But now he's staying for senior year so he can play baseball at Bayport."

Bayport? I didn't dare make eye contact with Jessie again. So, he'd be going to high school with us. Big deal.

The Jeep turned and bumped up the driveway into the garage. Kai and Jessie hopped out and grabbed the pizzas as I followed, holding two trays of drinks. A large painting propped against the wall in the garage caught my eye as I walked past. It was an abstract—a pretty decent one. I hadn't seen it before. Jessie's mom's chronic redecorating efforts were definitely in full swing.

Still studying the painting, I kept walking, my feet guiding me toward the back door. I liked the red up above, but I wasn't so sure about that splash of orange in the corner.

Just as I turned to step into the house, a blur of white smashed into my face—and crushing pain rushed in.

The door—the door had just *hit me in the nose*. I stumbled backward as one tray of drinks dropped, sending ice and soda splashing across the garage floor. The other tray I managed to set down before grabbing my face.

Jessie and Kai rushed back through the door. "Are you okay?" Jessie cried, reaching out to steady me.

"I'm so sorry!" Kai exclaimed. "Are you okay?"

My eyes watered as the pain radiated and pulsed through my nose. I tried to speak but found myself unable to manage a word—every ounce of my effort was focused on trying not to cry.

"Let's get you some ice," Jessie said. She guided me into the back hallway as I attempted to blink the pain away, but I quickly stopped short at the sight of the guys down at the end of the hall. They were still sitting in the living room with the music blaring, and every one of them turned to look at me. I clutched my nose tighter, trying even harder to fight back the tears. *Don't announce it.*

"The door slammed into her nose," Jessie's voice answered the question mark on their faces. She turned to me. "We'll get some ice, okay?"

Turning out of the hall to escape their stares, I stepped into Jessie's bedroom, my hand still covering my face. Out of the corner of my eye, I caught a glimpse of Leo. What was he doing striding down the hallway toward me? I sat down on the floral bedspread as my eyes darted to the doorway.

Leo rounded the corner into the bedroom. "You okay?" He squinted at me.

I nodded, glancing at my hand to check for blood. Relieved to find none, I rubbed the bridge of my nose and tried to smile. He came a little closer, tilting his head to inspect my face. I shifted my weight. The three feet of space between us felt more like three inches.

"How much does it hurt?" he asked. He sounded so genuine. I looked sideways, only able to think about the discomfort his stare was giving me. *How ironic.* All those days in middle school when I'd eye him from far away, wishing he would notice me for more than just a passing 'hey,' and now his sudden attention had surprised me to the point of stupidity. I couldn't answer. Heat burned into my cheeks, and I closed my eyes in a feeble attempt to make it stop.

To my relief, Jessie arrived through the doorway holding two small bags of ice and a washcloth. She stepped in front of Leo and positioned one of the bags onto my nose. Awkwardly, I tried to hold it in place. My eyes darted over to Leo. That look of chivalrous concern was still on his face.

Jessie sat next to me. "Are you okay?"

"I think so." I nodded, relieved that the pain had finally started to subside.

"Hey, Jessie?" Isaiah's deep voice called out from the kitchen.

"Be there in a sec!" she shouted.

In one deliberate movement, Leo took the extra ice and washcloth out of Jessie's hands. "I can help her."

Jessie's gaze shot to me and lingered for a quick moment before she left. All I could do was stare wide-eyed at the now empty doorway.

Leo gently took the bag from my nose and wrapped the ice in the washcloth. "This will be more comfortable," he said, eyeing my nose like an expert. "It doesn't look swollen at all. That's good." He put the ice into my hand and helped guide it back to my face.

It was not possible to feel any more un-pretty than at this moment. Pain and embarrassment had now mingled into one big, uncomfortable feeling. But another feeling was creeping up. I stole another glance at him. He looked like a Hollywood film star from the 1950's—chiseled, with a squinty stare.

I summoned the nerve to look into his eyes and finally spoke. "Thanks, I think I'm okay." My attraction clashed with my desire to hide. Suddenly, I wanted him to go away and stay all at the same time.

His brown eyes locked onto mine, and his mouth turned up at the corners. Was he enjoying my embarrassment? I had no choice but to laugh. "What?" I asked, pulling the ice away from my face.

He grinned and sat down next to me. "Dove, you need to keep the ice on it," he said, placing it back onto my nose.

The gentle way he said my name made my heart race faster, and I searched his face, drinking in its sincerity. His deep gaze somehow made me feel safe, and his lips seemed to be just waiting to… kiss me.

All at once, my enamored thoughts screeched to an abrupt stop.

No way.

My stomach twisted into a painful knot. How could I have fallen for the sensitive, caring act? Was I really lame enough to get all dreamy-eyed over a few sweet words and a pack of ice? There was no way I was going to end up as one of his conquests. With the ice still held to my nose, I stood with as much dignity as possible.

"Thanks, I'm fine now." I lowered the ice and looked straight into his dark, concern-filled eyes, shooting him a glare. "I have to go."

Chapter 2

> "And what a crush I had on you."
> -Sabrina Fairchild

Sabrina

Saturday morning, I pulled up to work in my stepmom's car, my head brimming with thoughts from the night before. The image of Leo's face floated in my mind, and I considered how much it had changed since those long-ago elementary and middle school days. Jessie was right, of course. He had been my very first crush. I still remembered that fluttery feeling I'd get from watching him stand in front of the class to share his state report in the fifth grade. Montana. He'd done it on Montana. And every time he looked at the class he'd smile in a shy, charming way. It was endearing and sweet—and so different from on the playground, where he seemed like just another rough, regular boy. By sixth grade, my tiny crush had turned into a huge one, but middle school made him cocky. All the admiring-girl attention turned his charm into arrogance. By the time he moved to Arizona at the end of eighth grade, I'd pushed away my secret feelings and refused to think of him anymore.

I shielded my eyes from the sun beaming in through the windshield. So much time had passed since then. His unexpected appearance and sudden interest in me last night had thrown me for a second, but it was understandable. Maybe the stress of the art show had taken its toll on me. Winning had become hugely important.

I slammed the car door closed and forced myself to focus on the day's work. There would be plenty to do. Aunt Gail worked with countless interior decorators, and keeping up with their designer demands kept the gallery more than busy.

"Dove!" My aunt's lyrical voice called out as I stepped into the gallery. Her tall figure strode into the front room with an armload of frames and matting. "The Miro lithograph is being picked up for approval today, okay?" Her blonde hair bobbed in perfect unison as she gave me a cheerful nod.

My aunt's flawless posture and pronunciation were as Audrey-esque as any woman could hope for. I always chalked it up to her years spent in Europe. But whatever the reason, I secretly wished that the poise she exuded would somehow rub off on me just by being around her. After all, we *were* related. If she could attain it so effortlessly, then it shouldn't be so difficult for me to achieve, either.

"Oh, and those need frames," she added, pointing to a stack of botanical prints. "Let's use gold."

THE MORNING FLEW BY, with me answering the gallery phone and helping the handful of clients who came into the showroom. At noon, I stepped outside and made my way down the bay-front boardwalk to Angelo's Café. Boat docks jutted up next to the waterfront shops and restaurants in the busy marina. Farther up, the stone bridge led to the homes on Lido Island.

The door to the café jingled when I pushed it open. "Hey, Angelo," I called out. The usual rich smell of coffee greeted me, along with Angelo's smiling face.

"*Buon Giorno!*" Angelo boomed in his deep voice. "How is my little *da Vinci* today?"

I pursed my lips and grinned. There was no use objecting to his ridiculous compliments, he'd just go on about it longer. "I'm fine, thanks."

He leaned over the counter and pointed a finger at me, nodding emphatically. "Yes, you are. You are a fine *artista*. What are you painting lately?"

"Oh, well, I was working on the Balboa Ferry, actually."

"Ah, yes! You were?" he beamed. "I want to see this latest masterpiece! You must bring it in. We will hang it next to the other one—I keep telling you," he continued in his thick Italian accent, "I need another one!"

I looked over my shoulder at the painting of Big Corona beach hanging on the wall next to the window. Foamy waves crashed along the shoreline, and little striped umbrellas stood crooked in the sand. As I eyed my own creation, I checked a surge of unexpected pride. Once in a while that happened. Just once in a while I'd see my own painting and not judge it harshly; I'd actually admire it. I shook my head. "I can't, Angelo. I'm entering the new one in the Orange County Fair today."

Angelo's leathery face brightened. "Ah!" He arched his eyebrows. "You will win for sure. And when you do, we will hang it with its ribbon right up there!" he said, pointing to a blank space on the wall.

My stomach flipped. That was the thing. It all depended on your definition of win. The division-winner ribbon or Best of Class would be great, but what I really needed was to win Best of Show—the best of all youth divisions combined. And that would not be easy. I had managed to win my division in tenth grade, and that had been a miracle. The chances of taking first prize were pretty slim.

With sandwiches dangling from a bag on my arm, I made my way back through the sunshine toward the gallery. The wind blew across the water, and I eyed the handful of boats bobbing on the bay. They looked so jittery out there—kind of like how I felt right now. I hadn't even wanted to think about the contest, much less *talk* about it with Angelo. *Just go with the flow*, I told myself. If the boats could jerk around out there without going under, then so could I.

My back pocket buzzed.

How's work? Jessie's text stared back at me.

Ok. Where are you?

You really need to ask? Beach!

Of course. Pretty much everybody spent their Saturdays at the beach but me. Still, the gallery job was worth the sacrifice. The beach could wait for Sundays.

Leo's here.

I blinked. For a brief moment, I pictured him. Tan. No shirt. Gorgeous as ever. No doubt he was flirting with every bikini body on the sand.

So? I returned.

Fire pits at Big Corona tonight. Wanna come?

For a split second, I considered it.

Can't. Fair entries are due tonight.

18

A LIGHT BREEZE BLEW across the empty fairgrounds as I crossed over the grass field toward the exhibition buildings.

It's a good entry, I told myself in an attempt to soothe my nerves. It was close to dark now, but I had purposely waited for the end of the day in order to be closer to the nine p.m. deadline. That way most of the entries would already be turned in. I'd be able to size up the competition... including Piper.

Piper. Her division win last year really had me freaked out. It had come as such a shock. After five years of placing ahead of her, her oil on canvas of a vase filled with flowers had beaten me out. Bested by a bouquet. I had to admit, though—it *was* pretty good. And in fairness, the entries were initially judged on how well they met a standard rather than how they compared to other entries. I rolled my eyes. Come to think of it, that was even more depressing.

The courtyard area outside Exhibition Building Fourteen was quiet and almost empty. A sign that read *Youth Fine Arts* fluttered against the large, arching entryway as I walked underneath, toting my watercolor under my arm.

A few people milled about in the huge hallway, and I stopped in the center of it, searching out the official sign-in desk. Off to the right, the aisles of already-hung entries loomed, but I pulled my gaze away, forcing myself to walk forward.

The woman behind the large reception desk nodded as I handed over my painting. A feeble smile masked my pounding heart and shallow breath as I completed the paperwork, while out of the corner of my eye the aisles of entries called to me. I signed my name and pushed the application across the desk, eager to go. Time to check out the competition.

Spinning around, I found myself face to face with Piper. Her perfect, Audrey-shade of brunette hair fell past her shoulders in rounded curls, and she tossed them with a flick of her head. I smoothed my own blonde waves with one hand in a self-conscious effort to compose myself.

"Hey, Dove." A smile crossed her face. It was halfway friendly.

"Hey." I forced a smile, certain it had nervous written all over it. My heart beat faster. I glanced down at the painting in her arms and stopped breathing. It was a watercolor. Of Newport Bay. And it was good.

I somehow sputtered, "Good luck," and then stepped around her, heading toward the huge doorway, now altogether ignoring the aisles of other entries. Piper had painted a seascape. She never painted seascapes. She always painted a still life—urns with tulips or bowls filled with apples. But she never painted seascapes! That was *my* thing, and she knew it. I felt a twinge of guilt between my waves of anger. Of course, anyone could paint whatever they wanted. No one owned the seawater. Still, it seemed incredibly sneaky of her to throw a curveball like that.

Curveball. The word reminded me of Leo. It really was surprising that he played baseball now. He seemed so serious about it, too. I pictured him in his uniform, throwing a ball and swinging a bat. He was probably a great player. I stopped myself. Yes, that was exactly what he was—*a player*. Why did my mind keep wandering to him?

Shrugging off my annoying thoughts, I picked up

my pace through the paved promenade and began to cut across the grassy field toward the parking lot. I was just stressed, that was all. The whole art show thing had me feeling crazed and vulnerable. I rubbed my forehead and squeezed my eyes shut, trying to forget the image of Piper's painting. Next Saturday the fair would open and results would be posted. One week. I'd have to wait one more week for my sanity to return.

Chapter 3

"I MUST SAY, THE MIND REELS..."
-HOLLY GOLIGHTLY

Breakfast at Tiffany's

I pressed my forehead to the glass the same way I'd done when I was little, mesmerized by the baby chicks inside the incubator. The fair's opening-day madness buzzed all around me, but I kept myself focused on the small puffs of yellow fluff inside the warm glass box. The simple exhibit was my own personal highlight of the fair every year. The tiny birds pecked and poked their way through the cracked eggs until finally shedding their broken shells, only to eventually scurry together in circles, making tiny peeping sounds.

"Knew I'd find you here."

I jumped at the voice in my ear and turned, almost bumping into Jessie.

"You okay?" She studied me.

"Of course, why?" I shrugged.

She frowned. "It's me, remember?"

I glanced back at the baby birds and let out a breath. "I really should've painted something different," I said, not moving my stare from the scampering chicks.

"Stop second-guessing yourself," Jessie said as she wrapped her arm around my shoulder and steered me outside the large barn exhibit. Together, we walked through rows of food stands and tents, weaving our way toward the art building while she distracted me with details of her birthday party. "Practically half the senior class is coming, so my mom finally said yes to having a band. I told her if everyone's dancing outside it would be way better than just sitting around, messing up the house."

I caught sight of Building Fourteen. A crowd of people was forming outside the large archway. "What time is it?"

Jessie fumbled for her phone. "Nine fifty-five."

"They won't open the doors till ten."

"Hang in there." She squeezed my elbow. "Five more minutes."

I drew in a breath, closed my eyes, and tried to summon the image of Audrey's self-confident face on my bedroom wall. *Poise. Composure. Poise.*

"Hey, Dove!" a voice called out from somewhere in the swarm of waiting people.

I stood on my toes, straining to see who it was. At the edge of the crowd, Kai smiled, waving what looked like a large, white piece of paper over her head. Kai's other hand was clasped onto Clive's as she pulled him through the crowd. I stared, wide-eyed. Behind Clive, a dark-haired guy trailed along, looking straight in my direction. Leo.

I spun at Jessie. "What are they doing here?"

Jessie shrugged and gave her best it's-not-my-fault look. "Kai asked me about it. What was I supposed to say?"

"Anything! I don't know! They can't be here!" I fixed my eyes on the ground and tried to steady myself. I was about to find out what a panel of judges thought of my work. The last thing I needed was an audience right now. Especially this one.

Jessie eyed my look of horror. "Okay... okay," she repeated with only a moment to spare. She leaned in to whisper into my ear. "I'll get rid of them."

Kai stepped alongside us, fluttering the white paper in front of our faces. "Hi guys!" Her voice was breathless. "Look what Clive and I had done!" she said, beaming.

Clive and Leo joined the circle as Jessie and I examined the paper together. The words *CLIVE and KAI* were scribbled at the top in cartoony letters, and below was a caricature drawing of the two. Shades of yellow highlighted Clive's long surfer hair against Kai's shiny black bob. Their large, smiling heads seemed to barely balance on top of their funny, miniature bodies. It really was adorable.

"Cute!" Jessie exclaimed.

I nodded and attempted a smile, then glanced in Leo's direction only to find him smiling at me.

"Hey," he said, friendly as ever. "How's your nose?"

"Fine—thanks," I added. I blinked away, trying my best not to be swayed by his dimples. Why was he here? Why were any of them here? I stared at Jessie, deep in conversation with Kai, and wondered when the get-rid-of-them part was going to happen. At that moment, the huge doors to the building slowly swung open, and the large swarm of people began to push forward.

Startled, Jessie snapped her head toward me and then back to Kai. "So, anyway, uh, Dove and I are going to check out her art thing and, um, maybe we'll meet up with you later?"

Kai shook her head. "No, that's okay. We'll just come with you. We want to check it out, too."

I could feel the tenseness in my entire body and I cursed it, wanting more than ever not to reveal how nervous I really was. *Awesome.* They could all participate in my artistic demise.

The movement of the crowd forced us closer to the doorway. "No, really," Jessie tried again. "It's pretty boring." She glanced at Clive and Leo. "The guys will probably hate it."

"No," Kai insisted. "It was Leo's idea to come, actually."

My eyes widened at Kai's words, but I continued to stare straight ahead as I stepped under the archway into the cool building. Leo's footsteps echoed directly behind me. I was sure they were his, and I was sure I could feel the weight of his stare on the back of my head.

Off to the right, the maze-like formations of display walls began to fill with people milling around, checking out the artwork and the ribbon-winning entries.

I turned to Jessie, ignoring the others. "I don't know where mine is. We have to search for it," I said, my voice almost at a whisper.

The distressed look on Jessie's face was enough of an apology. I shook my head, trying to let it go. "Forget it, let's just find my painting." We rounded the first corner and took in the sight of row after row of displayed artwork. Down the aisle, a green ribbon was pinned next to an entry.

Jessie leaned into me. "What does the ribbon look like again? The one you want?"

"It's white with purple around the edges," I answered. "That green one over there means it's a Judges' Choice— kind of like an honorable mention."

The judging system used at the Orange County Fair

went beyond the typical blue, red, and white ribbon standards. After class winners were sorted, ribbons were given for Best of Class, Best of Division, and Best of Show. "It will say Best of Show on it," I whispered, not wanting the others to hear. I glanced backwards, but they were no longer behind us. Down and across the aisle, Clive was holding hands with Kai. Leo was nowhere to be seen.

I turned another corner, now pulling Jessie behind me and scanning each wall for my watercolor. My heart hammered as we passed entry after entry, rounding endless twisting corners. I hadn't found my painting yet, but I hadn't seen an entry with the coveted ribbon on it, either. There was still a shred of hope.

"Uh-oh." Jessie stopped, looking over to her left.

I spun around and fixed my stare in the same direction. Across the aisle stood a proud-looking Piper in front of her painting of the bay. On the wall beside it, a white ribbon was pinned. I squinted to see the color of its ruffled edge, but Piper stood in animated conversation, blocking my view.

This was it. A sick feeling surged into my stomach. Piper laughed and tossed her hair, moving just enough for me to catch a glimpse of the top edges. Yellow.

"It's a Best of Division ribbon." I said, zombie-like.

"What does that mean?"

"It means she won first place for our age group." I swallowed. Piper had a ribbon. A good one. Heck, any ribbon was hard to win. I clenched my jaw and fought back the surge of emotion. How did I think I could possibly win Best of Show? It seemed so lame and unattainable now. It was ridiculous. I'd tried too hard. The need to find my painting and put myself out of my misery had grown to the point of crazy now.

"C'mon, let's find yours," Jessie said, pulling my arm.

I stopped her. "I think she saw us."

"So?"

I bit my lip. The tenseness now almost paralyzed me. "We should probably go congratulate her."

Jessie pushed my shoulder, shoving me away. "You go look for your painting. I'll congratulate her."

I stumbled away down the long aisle. Hadn't I seen all the artwork at this point? It had never taken this long to find my entry in years past. It also seemed like there were more entries than ever before. I looked again at a charcoal drawing of a horse and rider hanging beside me. Yes, I had seen that one already. Could I have passed my own painting in the craziness of it all? How was that possible?

Forcing myself to walk forward, I turned yet another corner and then stopped abruptly. A few feet ahead stood Leo with his back turned. Directly in front of him hung my watercolor of the Balboa Ferry. Several people lingered around it, looking on. With his hands in his pockets Leo looked over his shoulder and turned to face me, revealing a white ribbon pinned on the wall beside him.

"Congratulations," he said, squinting at me. He pointed to the ribbon. It had a purple ruffled edge. "I think this means you won."

Chapter 4

"SWEETNESS AND DECENCY."
-PRINCESS ANN

Roman Holiday

Outside my bedroom window, the water in the bay slowly faded to a navy darkness. It was hard to believe the day was already over. Instead of basking in my amazing win from the day before, I'd spent my entire Sunday preoccupied with one thing: Leo. The way he'd shown up to the contest and searched out my entry was... well, it was surprising. And there had been absolutely no evidence of those hotshot pretenses I hated so much, which now robbed me of any ammunition for despising him. It was hard to admit, but it seemed like he genuinely cared.

For about the hundredth time, I mulled over the moment when I realized I'd won. The room had whirled around me as I stepped forward to acknowledge my painting. The chaos of the moment and the complete and utter relief of having won the best ribbon of the show must have stripped me of my usual inhibitions, because in the midst of the many congratulations from

28

bystanders, Leo was the person my eyes came to rest on. Leo's face was the only one to anchor my smile on in a sea of unfamiliar faces. He just stood there, grinning and congratulating me with the rest of the group, and in my outright elation I reached over, put my arms around his neck, and hugged him.

I hugged him.

And he hugged me back. In fact, he made it quite clear that he liked it. I distinctly remembered being the first one to let go of the hug, and the happy expression that he wore without the tiniest shred of embarrassment. I, on the other hand, panicked at the warmth that began to tingle into my cheeks. My heart raced, and somehow I managed a "thanks" before Jessie saved the day, showing up just in the nick of time and distracting everyone with her loud whoops of joy.

I picked up the remote and pushed the play button. Audrey's enormous doe eyes peeked out from underneath her black hat with its huge rim. Fortunately, there was an Audrey film for every mood, and watching her as laid-back Holly Golightly in *Breakfast at Tiffany's* was the ideal choice in my crazed state.

All of the vintage-Hollywood Sunday matinees my mom had carted me to through the years had left their mark, but it was Audrey who stood out the most. Her charm and vulnerability made her totally relatable, and with her knack for fashion and her great sense of humor, I found her as irresistible to admire as my mom had. *Roman Holiday. Breakfast at Tiffany's. Sabrina.* My mom's worn copies of our three favorite classics, stacked in a perfect pile inside the cabinet, were always at the ready, waiting to be played late at night or at some random moment in need of inspiration.

I huddled into my cushioned window seat as Holly

perched on her own windowsill, guitar in hand, singing "Moon River." Who could successfully sing a love song to the water? Only Audrey. There was something seriously liberating about her. She had no problem owning her power or taking risks—two things I both admired and envied. Of course, there was Audrey as her movie characters, and then there was real-life Audrey as herself—but both were amazing. Maybe that was what was so great about her. She was a timeless, classic force to be reckoned with, both on and off the screen.

I pushed the button on the remote, fast-forwarding to the kissing-in-the-rain scene. It was hands-down my favorite part of the whole movie. Holly and Paul stood locked in a kiss, soaking wet, with a drenched orange tabby cat wedged between them and "Moon River" playing in the background. When it came to famous romantic endings, it didn't get much sweeter than this one.

I stared out the window at the dock floating on the water and wondered what Audrey would think of Leo. Would she give in to the magnetic pull of a guy she'd once fallen for, or refuse to trust a guy with a track record?

"Dinner!" The high-pitched sound of my stepmom calling was a welcome interruption for once. I headed downstairs to the dining room as the smell of something good wafted in from the kitchen.

I messed Griffin's hair as I sat down next to him. "Hey you, what'd you do today?"

He grinned and pushed my hand away. "Lacrosse practice."

"Lacrosse, huh? Wow that's... great." I studied his little face. His big-toothed smile made him look so much older now than the six-year-old boy who had moved in just four years ago.

Patty and my dad had married only a year and a half after my mom died—something I still hadn't quite wrapped my head around. But it had always been easy to love Griffin, with his huge green eyes and little freckled face.

"Lacrosse is very cool." I winked at him and then checked the deep-down annoyed and slightly jealous feeling that arose. Lacrosse? I distinctly remembered asking to play lacrosse when I was thirteen. But somehow that never happened. No doubt my stepmom considered it a boy sport—not that she would ever dare say so. For a motivational fitness instructor with more muscles than the average guy, it was surprising how eighteenth-century Patty could be when it came to these things. Still, her obsession with all things fitness worked in my favor. She didn't mind letting me borrow her car here and there since running or cycling to the gym and back was just an added workout.

The door to the kitchen swung open, and Patty sailed through in her pink yoga clothes holding two platters of food. My aunt followed close behind with a large dish of vegetables. I stood and reached for one of the platters, placing it on the table as everyone chatted and settled in around the table. The knotted feeling in my stomach eased at the tiny surprise of having my aunt join us for Sunday dinner. Aunt Gail would get my mind off Leo and onto something important and interesting, like an art auction in Prague or something. Any subject she brought up would be more than welcome.

My aunt served herself a scoop of green beans and glanced in my direction. "So, have you made any progress in the college-hunting department?"

Any subject but that one.

I gulped down a mouthful of potatoes and braced myself for the onslaught. Immediately, my dad jumped on the gotta-go-to-college-in-Chicago-just-like-me bandwagon, while my stepmom chimed in with the frugal benefits of staying in California.

Aunt Gail looked sideways at me, and I shook my head at her as discreetly as possible. Not now. Now was not the time.

She took a sip from her water glass, ignoring me. "You know, Dove and I have talked a lot about this, and I really think you should reconsider the idea of her studying art in Europe. Parsons Paris is ideal for what she wants to do." My dad stopped chewing and eyed his sister across the table, but Aunt Gail just shook her head, dismissing his frown. "Living abroad is exactly what she needs at this time in her life. And, as an artist, there's no better choice than Paris."

"But alone?" Patty ran her fingers along the slicked-back hair above her ear. More often than not, her taffy blonde hair was pulled into a bun so tight that even a wisp wouldn't dare escape. "She'll only be eighteen." My stepmom flashed an exasperated smile. "Not to mention the added expense of going to school in Europe."

Aunt Gail set down her fork. "Patty, she's completely capable. And I don't know if she's told you, but she's applying for an achievement scholarship."

My dad cleared his throat. "Gail... that's not an option," he grumbled.

"Actually, it is an option, Rick." My aunt turned her head to him. "In fact, it's a very viable option for her—"

"There are plenty of great art schools here in the U.S.," he interrupted. "It's not necessary to go halfway around the world."

Silence filled the dining room as my dad and Aunt

Gail stared at each other across the flickering candles.

My dad cleared his throat again. "Besides, Dove's got her sights on the Art Institute of Chicago, don't you, Dove? With my connections, it's practically a done deal."

All eyes turned to me. Why did Aunt Gail insist on bringing this up tonight? Of course she was trying to help, but I was in no way prepared to have this conversation. It wasn't time yet. I needed to actually get the scholarship before I brought it up and lobbied for it. Now I had no choice but to downplay the whole thing. There was no way we would ever get my dad to budge by forcing the issue anyway.

I straightened in my chair and nodded diplomatically. "Yeah, I like the Art Institute." I flicked an apologetic glance toward my aunt. "Parsons in Paris would of course be wonderful, but..." I eyed my stepmom and smiled. "Actually, I've done some research on the San Francisco Art Institute, and it's pretty great, too."

"Well, there you go." My stepmom grinned as though all was right with the world. "Gail," she turned to my aunt, "did you know that Griffin has started playing lacrosse? Griffy, tell Aunt Gail about it."

As Griffin began to rattle on about sticks and helmets, my phone buzzed in my jeans pocket, but with the clinking of forks and all the talking, no one else heard it. I slid the phone from my back pocket and read the text under the table.

Fire pits tonight?

Jessie, of course. I thought for a moment, unsure what to do. My phone buzzed again.

Come on. Summer's almost over.

Would Leo be there? I began to type the question when another text buzzed through.

Leo's coming. Ahem. Let's not kid ourselves. I saw

the hug.

I moved my thumbs over the keys. *I need to talk to you.*

A mere three seconds had passed when my phone buzzed once more. *I know you do. Tonight at the beach. Pick you up at 7?*

I looked down the length of the taupe dining room wall to the grandfather clock. Six twenty. Leo would be there. That was a reason *not* to go, not a reason *to* go, I reminded myself. Still, the curious fascination with him just wouldn't go away.

Ok.

Everyone's loud conversation continued, and I took another bite of my dinner as my phone buzzed one last time.

Thought so. xo

JESSIE'S JEEP ROUNDED THE grassy corners on the cliffs of Corona Del Mar. The last wedge of sun had dropped below the horizon, but bits of red glowing light still lingered in the sky, suspending it somewhere between day and darkness. Down below, waves crashed onto the shore and white peaks slapped against the rock jetties as the gulls made their final dives into the surf.

The Jeep turned and descended the steep road to the beach. I laughed as Jessie gripped the wheel with one hand and gestured in her comical way with the other, relaying the details of her latest debate team argument.

When we climbed out of the Jeep and headed toward the sand, I looked over at her. We still hadn't talked about Leo. I opened my mouth to raise the subject but held back again.

"Well, they're definitely here." Jessie pointed to a blue truck as we walked past. "That's Leo's."

I took a second look. It was an older-model, vintage Bronco. With its heavy grill and thick-treaded tires, it looked like the quintessential guy car.

Jessie reached out, hooking her arm into mine. "Speaking of which. About Leo—spill."

I took a deep breath, letting it out slowly. "I'm not sure what to think. He acted completely interested that night at your house, but I just, you know, assumed it was Leo being, well... Leo. You know, like in middle school. One second he was hot on a girl, and the next, he'd just drop her."

Jessie looked out at the horizon. "Yeah. He was quite the ladies' man. It does seem like he's grown up a bit, though. I don't know. Maybe he's different now..." She turned, pulling me toward the rocks to the right. "This way. They're over at Pirate's Cove."

Several people were climbing over the large rock formations separating the little bay cove on the far side from the ocean waves. I followed along behind Jessie, both of us carefully choosing our footing on the jagged, sandy rocks.

Considering the idea of giving him a chance made my stomach flutter, forcing me to face the fact that I definitely still found him more than intriguing. But I couldn't just blindly trust him, could I?

One foot slid on a rock, and I caught myself. Black ballet flats probably weren't the best idea right now, even if they were the best Audrey shoes ever. I slipped them off and continued barefoot up the sandy trail. Audrey. She would've known exactly what to do in this situation. And even if she hadn't, she'd have probably just figured something out right on the spot—some kind of plan.

I stopped at the top of a boulder to catch my breath. That was it... I needed a plan. Staring out across the jetty, I breathed deeply, watching as three seagulls flapped their wings into the darkening sky. I decided almost instantly. *Three things.* I would simply watch him carefully, and if he somehow showed himself to be a nice, decent guy at least three times, I would consider the idea of showing my interest. On the other hand, if any of that past jerkishness reared its ugly head, I'd walk away and forget about him forever. I clenched my jaw and started to negotiate my way over the rocks again. It wasn't the best plan in the world, but it was something to go on at least.

Reaching the opposite side, I hopped down onto the sand, my flats still in hand. It had been years since I'd been to Pirate's Cove. Shallow caves peeked out of the rocks on that side of the jetty. In the distance, small circles of orange bonfires already glowed in the sand.

I watched as Jessie ran ahead toward a cluster of kids. Kai and Clive were chatting with another couple. Beside them, a bunch of kids made up a large circle. I spotted Isaiah. And there was Leo. My stomach did a flip. He was wearing jeans and a red Angels baseball jersey that clung to his chest in the breeze.

A girl with light blonde hair stood next to him, her long curls falling in effortless, perfect ringlets. She laughed and touched his arm, trying her best to steal his attention from the group discussion. Leo didn't react. Laughter broke out from the group and he turned, walking toward the empty fire pit where Isaiah had begun to pile bits of driftwood and newspaper.

"Leo!" the blonde called out. "You can't leave me! They're making fun of me!"

Oh please. Could her attempt for his attention be more desperate? Leo looked over his shoulder, smiled politely, and continued to ignore her as he walked away.

That's One.

I made my way toward the circle as Isaiah and Leo worked together to start the fire. A large flame burst upward, and they both sprang out of its reach, erupting in laughter. I stepped alongside Jessie to join the circle and, unable to resist the urge, looked over my shoulder in Leo's direction. With a small turn of his head he caught sight of my glance. His huge smile faded into thoughtful seriousness when his dark eyes fixed on me, and he nodded, shooting me his signature squint.

Like a magnet, the group was drawn to the flames of the bonfire. Leo and a few of the guys ran along the shoreline, tossing a football back and forth while music blared from beside the fire pit.

I sat on a blanket in the sand near some of the others, and Isaiah sat down next to me, shaking the sand out of his short, black hair. "Hey."

I scooted over to make room for him. "Hi."

"So, I heard you won an art show or something," he said with a grin.

I smiled at his frank, casual way. It was so much like Jessie's. Too bad they had broken up again because he was super nice... and perfect for her. The two of them had been together most of junior year, and I'd teased Jessie more than once that between his brown complexion and her auburn hair, their future kids were bound to be beautiful. "Yeah, it was a contest at the fair," I answered.

"That's awesome. What was it a picture of?" His eyebrows sprang up. "Wait, no, let me guess... um, a rainbow?"

I shook my head and resisted the urge to roll my eyes.

"No? Okay, uh... a naked lady?"

I stifled a smile, dismissing his ridiculous guess with a wave of my hand.

"No?" He laughed. "Wait, I've got it. It was a bunch of splatters, like that one artist guy—Jack somebody..."

"Jackson Pollack. And no." I looked up as I laughed. At the shoreline, a woman was jogging past Leo and the guys. All at once, she darted sideways toward the water to avoid the path of their football, but suddenly lost her footing in the wet sand and stumbled. Leo shot forward, catching her just before she fell.

That's two. I looked sideways. Had he read my mind or something? Everything about him tonight seemed genuine and unselfish. My eyes settled on him again.

Isaiah waved his hand in front of my face. "Hello there? Didn't anyone teach you it's not polite to stare?"

I whipped my head around to find Isaiah studying me.

"Well, well, well. The way you left so fast the other night, I thought you weren't interested in Leo."

I pushed his shoulder with one finger. "That is none of your business," I said as I stood, heading toward one of the chairs filled with snacks. "And by the way, it was a painting of the ferry," I called out over my shoulder.

Isaiah bobbed his head up and down. "Ah. Uh-huh. Should have known—a sweet Newport Beach picture for a sweet Newport Beach girl."

I shot him a half-serious glare and sank my teeth into a marshmallow. No roasting necessary, especially at a time like this. Sweet. A description I never knew quite what to think of. Was it sweet in a good way? Like, you're-a-nice-person type of sweet? Or was it sweet in a lame way? As in, way-too-sugary-sweet, like this boring marshmallow? And why was Isaiah questioning me? Had Leo sent him to check out the situation? I sort of hoped so, but if I were to follow my own plan I still needed one more piece of evidence to prove Leo wasn't a jerk.

I watched as Jessie trotted up and plunked herself onto the blanket in my vacated spot next to Isaiah. He sized her up, and she quipped something at him I couldn't hear, smiling at him while brushing the sand from her legs. The chemistry between them was blaringly obvious. Why did they fight it?

Kai grabbed my arm and pulled me next to the fire. Most of the group was gathering around now, and I made a conscious effort not to look across the flames at Leo, who still seemed to be ignoring the blonde-ringlet girl.

"Hey, by the way," Kai said, turning to me, "we're going to the fair again on Thursday. Maybe you and Jessie can come."

'We' will include Leo. It was the first thought that sprang into my head, and I immediately nodded only to stop short. "Oh wait. I can't." Across the fire, Leo stopped talking. Was he listening to me? "I'm doing this charity event at my aunt's gallery."

Kai grimaced at me.

"No, it's pretty great, actually," I said. "It's this plein-air painting workshop for inner-city kids, to raise money and awareness."

"Plein-air?" Leo's voice rang out across the fire. "What's that?"

Startled, I turned to him. His eyes glinted in the light of the fire as he waited for my answer. "It's French. It means outdoors. The kids will be painting outside."

He nodded with a serious-looking stare, and his eyes lingered longer than necessary. I pulled my gaze back to Kai, who was now talking to the girl beside her.

A crisp breeze blew off the ocean, crackling the embers of the fire. Night had come, with its darkness slowly surrounding us. I huddled in closer to the flames, trying to escape the cold air.

Behind me, someone's feet sifted through the sand. I turned my head as a heavy, plaid blanket wrapped around my shoulders. Leo bent down toward me. "You're too close to the fire," he said, grabbing my elbow and pulling me backwards. "When the wind changes, the flames could burn you."

And there it was. *Three.*

The flannel shirt he'd thrown on was unbuttoned, and the wind flapped it open a little, revealing his red Angels jersey. He sat down beside me, leaving a large gap of empty space between us.

Time to be friendly. "So, you like the Angels." My own comfort level surprised me. It came out as a statement, not a question.

He laughed. "Favorite team. I've had this shirt for like three years. Got it with my dad at Angel Stadium."

"Kai says you're really good—that you'll probably be drafted next year." As soon as the sentence left my mouth, I wished I could take it back. I squirmed. Now he would think I'd been discussing him with everyone.

Leo shrugged, unfazed. "Yeah, I definitely hope to go pro." Nothing seemed to embarrass him.

On the other side of the fire, two people had started to make-out, their bodies practically entwined. I couldn't help glancing in their direction every few seconds. How could they just ignore everyone around them like that? They barely ever came up for air. I looked away, half of me annoyed and judgmental, the other half admiring the sheer boldness of it.

Leo looked sideways at them as they continued on, still oblivious to their audience. He tilted his head in their direction. "Does that bother you?"

"What?" I knew exactly what he was referring to, but his gutsy question surprised me.

His face stayed serious. "Them kissing like that."

I threw him my best casual expression and shrugged my shoulders. "No." I stared out at the ocean, my thoughts churning along with the waves. He sure was sure of himself.

"What are you thinking about?" he asked, his voice almost a whisper as he bent his head toward me.

I looked down, burying my feet deeper into the sand. "There's something about the beach at night—the coldness of the sand, the water, the darkness. I don't know—it's kind of magical."

Leo looked out toward the rushing water and pushed his hair out of his eyes with one hand. I watched as his palm trailed down the back of his head, stopping to clasp the back of his neck. "Damn. I was hoping maybe you were thinking about me."

I turned to take in his face. His right eyebrow fell lower than his left as his intense stare burned into me. I pursed my lips and held back a smile, not daring to tell him. *I was.*

Chapter 5

Sabrina

At the gallery on Tuesday I found myself stationed at the front desk, staring blankly at a wall of freshly framed botanical prints. The whole group was hanging out at Clive's house for the day, which had become a weekly routine when his mom was at work. Normally, I avoided going. A bunch of Bayport kids just sat around the swimming pool and blasted the stereo or played billiards inside at the pool table. But when Leo texted and asked me to meet him there, suddenly the whole thing sounded like something I might actually want to be a part of.

I swiveled in my chair and then grabbed my phone to check it for the hundredth time. Ten minutes past noon. At this rate, it would take forever to get to three o'clock. I let out a breath and scolded myself for being as crazy excited about him as I was.

"Dove?" Aunt Gail called out. "Hello... are you awake?" She entered the showroom from the back office.

I snapped myself out of my hypnotic stare. "Sorry."

"What's going on?"

I stood. "Nothing… nothing. I need to focus. What do you want me to work on?"

"Do you have something going on today?" She pressed for an answer. "Something you need to do?"

"No, it's okay. Tell me what you need—I'm ready to work."

She stopped and scanned the gallery. "You know, why don't you take off early today? There's not much happening around here. We're completely ready for Thursday's workshop. Go ahead and go."

I hesitated, arguing with myself. The right thing to do would be to stay—to prove my dedication and maturity. Be responsible and all that.

My aunt read my mind. "You're just filling in for me today anyway, and it turns out I don't really need the help after all." She shrugged at me and winked. "Go ahead and take the rest of the day off."

No more coercing was necessary. There seemed to be no end to the niceness of my aunt. I shot her my most grateful smile. "Thank you, Aunt Gail!" I grabbed my keys, threw two more thank-yous over my shoulder, and pushed my way out the front door.

A BUNCH OF CARS packed both sides of the street near Clive's house. I carefully steered my stepmom's Audi into the crowded, narrow driveway, pulling into a small space next to the fence alongside the backyard.

Noisy chatter greeted me when I opened the car door. I heard the distinct sound of Leo's deep laughter from over the fence, and my stomach fluttered. Loud shouts echoed through the yard, sounding more and more like the typical ruckus of a drinking game well underway. I stepped onto the bottom edge of the wood railing and poked my head over the fence to check it out.

Sure enough, a bunch of plastic cups filled with beer lined the patio table, and a group of kids was gathered around, tossing a ping-pong ball into the red cups. The laughter grew loud again as someone missed their throw.

At the sight of Leo, my mouth stopped halfway to a smile. He was sitting next to the table, turned toward a blonde girl sitting beside him. They were holding hands.

The girl from the beach.

Her ringlets waved in the breeze, and she leaned closer, giggling as she pulled him toward her. As if in slow motion, their lips met. I made an effort to blink.

Frozen and hoisted awkwardly onto the fence, my heart pounded faster with each second that ticked by. My brain reeled, trying to catch up with what my eyes told me.

Beside the pool, Isaiah turned his head in casual conversation and caught a glimpse of me. He immediately turned back around to get Leo's attention. "Leo!" he called out over the sound of laughter and talking.

Leo didn't hear it, and I continued to watch as the girl smiled and put her other hand on his knee. He laughed with her.

"Leo!" Isaiah called out again.

Leo kept on talking, oblivious to me. I wanted to hop down, but I just tightened my grip on the fence.

Isaiah tried a third time. "Leo!"

Leo turned, and my eyes locked with his. He stood

and began to scramble toward the gate before I finally let go of the fence and dropped down. Behind me, the gate creaked and banged as I stalked to my car and slid into the driver's seat.

Reaching out, he caught my car door before I could close it. "Dove, hey—it's not what you think."

I mustered up my most casual tone. "What?" I shrugged my shoulders, pushing the key into the ignition.

"Seriously, Dove—please don't leave."

I looked up at him, my face twisting with confusion. "Why do you care? You don't owe me anything. It's completely fine."

"No, I know, it's just—after we talked at the beach, I sorta thought, you know, you and I..." His voice trailed off, and he looked away, shaking his head.

Wow. He actually almost said it. I let out a scoff. "Yeah, I sorta thought that, too, but..." I flicked my gaze toward the fence and shrugged again. "I don't think so anymore."

His gaze dropped to the pavement as he quietly shut my door and stepped back. I made an effort not to look at him again as I put the car in reverse and backed down the driveway. Out of the corner of my eye I could see him still standing there, staring at me as I drove away.

I PULLED THE CAR to a stop beside the curb in front of Jessie's house and stared across the yard at the big tree bent over the fence. A tiny corner of the tree house was visible, and I watched as the leaves rustled in the wind around its wooden shape. What was I doing here? Jessie was at a debate meeting. There was no point in being

45

here. Still, somehow it was comforting and better right now than the thought of going home. Home. Such a little word. But its significance was so different now without my mom around to give it the meaning I wanted.

I sat with quiet surrounding me and blinked into the bright daylight. How ridiculous I must have looked peering over the fence. Ridiculous and naïve—and come to think of it, exactly like Audrey in *Sabrina*... always climbing trees to spy on William Holden dancing with his girlfriends at parties. It was cringe-worthy.

I drew in a deep breath, closing my eyes at the thought of it. At least I was in good company. But there was no getting around it, the whole incident screamed embarrassing and pathetic.

The stillness broke when my phone rang out. Jessie's name lit up the screen.

"Hi Jess."

"Hey. Isaiah called and told me you left Clive's without even going in."

Great. Everyone was talking about it. Of course they were. "Did he tell you why?"

"Leo."

"He was kissing that blonde girl." I let out a breath. "And I had just convinced myself that maybe he wasn't the player type anymore. Whatever. It's not like we were even dating anyway." I shook my head at the stupidity of it all. "It's okay, it was probably meant to happen so I could see his true inner jerk." I stared out at the tree house again.

"For what it's worth, Isaiah said that Clarissa was completely the aggressor."

"Clarissa?" How annoying. Even her name was sexy. "Who is she?"

"She's a junior. I looked her up. Let's just say she's

CHAUCER'S BOOKSTORE
3321 State St. Santa Barbara CA 93105
(805) 682-6787 Open 9-9 M-Sat, 9-8 Sun

Help launch Gregory Crouch's new book,
"Bonanza King" Thursday, June 28th @7pm

the kind of girl who gets three hundred likes when she posts a picture of a greasy cheeseburger." I groaned as Jessie continued. "I know, right? As if she would ever even touch a cheeseburger. Anyway, she definitely has a reputation for sleeping around. Isaiah said she was throwing herself at him."

"Whatever. I saw the kiss," I scoffed. "And he looked completely willing."

"Isaiah said he's bummed about it."

"Well, I don't really care, now, do I?"

Jessie paused. "Um... let's see, is no the right answer?"

I let out a laugh. "Yes! No is the right answer." I straightened in my seat. This was it. I'd wasted enough time on this guy.

"Great, so were going with... No, you don't care." Jessie chuckled. "Where are you?"

"In front of your house." I laughed. "I didn't feel like going home. I'm just sitting here, tempted to climb into the tree house."

Jessie was silent as a moment ticked by. "Let's do it!" Her voice came shouting out of the front door. I turned to see Jessie standing in the doorway, waving.

I climbed out of the car. "I thought you had debate today!"

She shrugged, smiling. "I thought *you* had to work."

Chapter 6

"THURSDAY? IS THIS THURSDAY? THURSDAY! OH NO, IT CAN'T BE!" - HOLLY GOLIGHTLY

"THURSDAY? IS THIS THURSDAY? THURSDAY! OH NO, IT CAN'T BE!"
- HOLLY GOLIGHTLY

Breakfast at Tiffany's

I rolled over in bed with a feeling of unease. Sunlight beamed through the bay window, and I sat up in bed, unable to shake the disturbing notion that something was different. Jessie's birthday party? No, that was Saturday night. Today was Thursday. A free day. Then what was bothering me? My breath caught. *The workshop.*

I squinted toward the digital clock, not wanting to know exactly how late I actually was. 10:08. *Oh no.* I sprang from the bed, grabbed my clothes from the closet, and threw them on as fast as possible. The workshop had started over an hour ago. I grabbed my phone and looked at it. Five messages. Vowing never to silence the thing again, I shoved it into my pocket and flew out of my bedroom without even a glance at Audrey's poster.

When I pulled my stepmom's car into the Lido Marina, my stress level had peaked. The sight of balloons waving and groups of easels set up outside the gallery made my stomach flip. That was supposed to be *my* job. I ran toward the gallery, weaving through the clusters of people who had gathered around to watch. Grade-school kids sat in front of each easel, moving their brushes across the canvases, looking completely absorbed in their works-in-progress.

I scanned the crowd for my aunt and then burst into the front door of the gallery. She turned, her eyes widening. "There you are!"

"I'm so sorry!" I blurted, trying to catch my breath. "I tried to call, but I only got your voicemail—"

My aunt nodded, slowing me down. "Well actually, we're coming along okay. We've got twelve kids, it looks like," she said, craning her neck to see the easels outside. "And just enough volunteers... thanks to your friend," she added.

I wrinkled my forehead. "What? What friend?"

She peered out the window again. "I think he said his name is Leo?"

I looked sideways, trying to take in the words. "Leo is here?"

She nodded. "Yes, he showed up at eight and helped me with the setup. I couldn't have done it without him."

"Wait. *Really*?"

My aunt shot me a confused frown, dismissing my question, and jumped right into her list of things that still needed to be done. "...And most importantly, make sure the kids are enjoying the experience," she finished with a nod.

Bobbing my head in agreement, I glanced out the windows in an attempt to see Leo, but with all the activity outside I couldn't spot him. I filled my arms with tubes of paint and then stopped for a moment, closing my eyes to picture Audrey's smiling face on my poster. *Poise. Confidence.* Breathing deeply, I shouldered the front door open and stepped outside.

I ignored the urge to scan the crowd for Leo's face, and instead stopped at the first few easels near the doorway to chat with people as I filled their palettes with more acrylics. The workshop had been well organized. To assist the kids, an adult volunteer sat beside each one to help them through the process. The whole thing had been perfectly planned by my aunt, who recruited several artists and friends from the art world every summer to volunteer as mentors for the outreach. I was supposed to have been one of them. I turned and looked over my shoulder at the group of easels alongside the boardwalk.

There he was.

Leo was sitting next to a boy and pointing out toward the water. Then he pointed to the canvas and said something. They laughed together.

I took another deep breath and headed straight in their direction, stopping beside their easel. "Hi."

Leo turned his head. His eyebrows sprang up. "Hey!"

I looked sideways and back again. "Um, thanks... thank you..."

"Oh, it's no problem," he said. He looked over at the boy beside him who had now stopped painting. "This is Evan, he's got some serious talent."

I smiled at the boy, who grinned again at Leo and then at me. He dipped his brush into the palette and continued painting.

I looked at Leo again. "So anyway, like I said, um, thanks so much... I can take over from here if you want," I said, compulsively pushing one side of my hair behind my ear.

"No way. Evan and I are buddies. You go ahead and work on whatever else needs to be done." He shot me his smile. "I've got this."

He didn't blink as I searched his face, trying to read him. He looked proud of himself, yet humble about it at the same time. Pretty smooth. I shifted my weight and nodded. "Okay." I handed him a couple tubes of paint and then pulled my eyes away from his as I headed toward the next occupied easel.

THE MORNING RACED BY as people milled through the boardwalk area and the kids worked at their canvases. I engaged with all the guests, the way my aunt had taught me, educating them about plein-air painting as an art therapy experience, and the importance of fostering the arts.

By noon, the event had ended and the crowd had cleared in front of the gallery, leaving a display of a dozen freshly painted masterpieces to line the boardwalk in front of the boat docks. Leo worked in silence alongside the last few volunteers, folding easels and carrying in the supplies. I watched him from a distance. All morning long I had analyzed his motive. It was clearly an attempt at forgiveness. He wanted a second chance, right? He was trying to prove himself worthy or something.

I bit the inside of my cheek. He was doing a pretty good job of it. Maybe giving him one more chance would be an okay thing to do. After all, it's not like I'd had any kind of claim to him or anything. And it *had* looked as if Clarissa had been throwing herself at him. Still, the thought of trusting him made my stomach churn.

I walked toward him, and he glanced in my

direction while lifting a chair onto a stack of others. "Hey," I offered.

"Hi." He rubbed the back of his head, and his hand traveled down to linger on his neck.

I was starting to recognize that neck move. He did it a lot. Especially when he seemed—what was it? Self-conscious? Nervous? I shifted my weight, trying my best not to actually feel badly for him now... or notice how incredibly gorgeous he looked with his arm flexed that way. "I just wanted to say thanks one more time. You really helped us out. I mean, you really helped me out... really..." *Really*? I breathed in to slow myself down. "So, how did you even know about this?"

"You were talking about it at the beach, remember?"

Of course. He sure had been paying attention. "Right. Well, thank you."

"No problem," he said, offering a half-squint smile. "I'm glad I could help." He glanced out at the water and then moved his gaze back to me. "Want to get some lunch or something?"

Before I could stop myself, I looked him up and down. I had to admit, it would be pretty cold-hearted to say no after what he'd done for me. And it was just lunch, after all. I drew in a breath and found a smile. "Okay."

THE BUSY LUNCH CROWD didn't stop Angelo from finding us a small table by the window.

He set silverware on our napkins as his voice boomed above the noise. "Ah yes! It is a beautiful day, no? And your art benefit has made us even busier than usual." He winked at me. "But I always have a table for

52

the *artista*."

I held back a wince, concealing it with a smile. What was I thinking coming here? Angelo meant well, but how could I play it cool when he was showering me with his *way* over-the-top praise? My eyes flitted to Leo, who was giving a casual nod to Angelo.

"Have you seen her artwork?" Angelo gestured to the painting on the wall nearby. "She painted that one." His head bobbed. "I'm telling you, she has a lot of talent, this girl."

Leo laughed, nodding in agreement. "Oh, I know. She just won the show at the fair."

Angelo's jaw dropped as his eyes went wide. "Why did you not tell me?" He tipped a pitcher, filling our glasses with water. "I knew you would win! Didn't I tell you?" He shook his head at Leo. "She doesn't know how good she is," he added as he turned and walked away.

Leo squinted. "Is it me, or is that the Italian waiter guy from *Lady and the Tramp*?"

I laughed as I pictured the cartoon chef with his white apron and huge mustache. Definitely a doppelgänger for Angelo. All that was missing was a bow tie and an accordion.

Leo smiled. "Seriously. I think that's him." He looked over his shoulder toward the kitchen. "We'll know for sure if he brings us a huge plate of spaghetti."

My smile faded at the thought of the famous spaghetti scene. Everyone knew how it ended—with one string of spaghetti and a kiss. Without realizing it, I had fallen right into his flirtatious trap. I moved my gaze to the boats out the window and then back to Leo again.

He cleared his throat. "Anyway… sounds like he might be your biggest fan."

I rolled my eyes. "You made it worse by mentioning the fair."

"You should be proud." His eyes sparkled at me as he took a sip of water. "Speaking of the fair, do you want to go on Saturday?"

Wait. We hadn't even eaten lunch yet, and he was asking to go somewhere together again? I grabbed my own glass of water just to have something to hold onto. "I thought everyone was going today."

He shrugged. "Some people did. A few of us are going Saturday though, since, you know, you and I couldn't make it today."

My stomach flip-flopped at the words 'you and I.' I liked the sound of it. *Stop it, Dove.* I could feel my wheels turning as I tried to resist the fact that my resolve was weakening. In truth, I knew exactly what was happening. I'd seen it go down in *Sabrina* about a hundred times. Audrey had fallen for Humphrey, and that fact would not go away no matter how much she ignored it.

I looked sideways. Half of me wanted to run to the bathroom so I could bang my head against the wall. No. There was no 'you and I,' and there was no 'fair on Saturday.' At least there shouldn't be. "I better not," I finally answered. "I need to help Jessie get her party ready."

Right away, the other half of me started to battle against the play-it-safe side, ready to give him a chance. All of a sudden, I wished I could take back my answer.

He shook his head at me. "Jessie told me she's going Saturday, before her party." He smirked as though he'd caught me now. "I'd really like you to go..." His eyes zeroed in on mine. "With me."

I pressed my lips together, unable to ignore the

whole unspoken thing any longer. It was time to just say it. "I don't know, Leo."

He leaned forward, ready as ever. "Why? Because of that girl at Clive's pool?"

I stared at him.

"I'm not a jerk, Dove."

I blinked, wanting to believe it.

"How can I convince you?" He lowered his eyes, glanced away for a moment, and then leaned in closer across the little table. "I'm just gonna say it." He paused, his eyes roving over my face. "I really like you, and I don't like anyone else."

His bluntness caught me off-guard, and I breathed out a laugh. "Well, wow," I blurted.

He rested his arms on the table, his face still serious. "What? I thought you artists were all about people expressing themselves."

I made an effort to hold back an approving smile. *Touché.* Man, he was charming.

He sat stone-faced, not moving his stare from mine. "So, what do you say?"

My breathing turned shallow. He may be smooth, but he was definitely putting it all out there. He was genuine. I could feel it somewhere deep inside. I matched his serious look with my own. "Okay. I say... I say yes."

Chapter 7

"LA VIE EN ROSE. IT IS THE FRENCH WAY OF SAYING, 'I AM LOOKING AT THE WORLD THROUGH ROSE-COLORED GLASSES.'"
-SABRINA FAIRCHILD

Sabrina

Alone at the kitchen counter on Saturday morning, I leaned my head on one hand and lifted my spoon above my cereal with the other, allowing the milk to splash like a waterfall back into the bowl. My stomach twisted at the thought of actually being together with Leo at the fair, and then Jessie's party that night. His words from two days before played out in my memory. *With me,* he'd said. I stirred my spoon in my cereal, swirling the milk in circles. *With me.*

"Morning, baby," my dad said, rounding the corner into the kitchen.

"Morning." My spoon slipped from my fingers, clinking against the bowl, and I fumbled for it, quickly scooping a large bite of soggy cereal into my mouth.

He picked up the newspaper off the kitchen table. "Jessie's party tonight?" he asked, sitting down.

"Mmhmm." I grabbed my bowl, heading to the sink.

"So..." he said, pausing.

I turned my head. Anytime my dad started a sentence with 'so,' it was never good.

"I hear you had a lunch date the other day." He unfolded his newspaper.

I froze. How did he know that? It wasn't like I was trying to keep it secret, but I hadn't talked about it with anyone.

He smiled knowingly. "Aunt Gail mentioned it."

Great. Thanks, Aunt Gail. I forced a nonchalant shrug in his direction.

He turned a page of the newspaper, scanning it. "So, who is he?"

Oh no. Oh no no no. I hadn't even thought about it. My dad was Mr. Old-Fashioned. He was going to ask to *meet* him, like he always tried to insist on when I went somewhere with a guy. It was archaic. Pure torture.

I rinsed my dish and answered as casually as possible. "His name's Leo. I don't know... he's more of a friend, really."

He scratched his mess of silvery hair, nodding, and I relaxed my grip on the dish.

"Going to work today?" he asked.

"No, I worked Thursday's benefit instead," I said, drying my hands on a dishtowel and heading toward the doorway.

"Where are you off to?"

I turned and gave him a laid-back smile. "The fair."

"Oh." He didn't move from behind his newspaper, and I held my breath as I stepped toward the door.

"With who?" he suddenly added, sending my heart sinking.

I turned again, facing him. "With Jessie, and Kai

and Clive, you know, that whole group."

"And Leo?" He looked up over his newspaper.

"Mmhmm," I said, ignoring his interest.

"I'd like to meet this guy."

I dipped my head sideways and gave up on the casual act. "That's completely awkward, Dad."

He raised his eyebrows. "What? Are you embarrassed of me?"

"No, it's just embarrassing in general." I rolled my eyes. "I seriously doubt Mom would have insisted on this."

I bit my cheek, regretting my statement immediately. If there was one thing my dad didn't like, it was telling him how my mom would have done things better. In fact, he didn't seem to be a fan of talking about her much at all anymore. He'd done okay when I was little, mentioning this or remembering that, but as each year rolled by, it seemed like we spoke of her less and less. I eyed his stiff expression and took a breath, readying myself to smooth it over. "It's just that it's antiquated. I mean, no one does that anymore."

He shrugged, his frown slowly disappearing. "I'm antiquated. Humor me." He winked.

"Seriously, Dad." I shook my head at him, wondering what it would be like if my mom were actually here to help. She would have known how to handle it with him. "It's not funny to me. We're just friends."

"You're going to the fair with him today, you went on a lunch date with him yesterday, and I assume you'll be with him at the party tonight." He pinned me to the wall with his stare. "Am I right?"

"Yes, but..." I sputtered.

"I'd like to meet him." He fluttered his paper back up in front of him. "Tonight. Before the party," he pronounced in his serious tone—the one that was impossible to argue with.

And everyone calls ME stubborn? I sneered as I headed out of the kitchen. There was no doubt where that trait had come from.

THE SUN BLAZED DOWN onto the crowded fairgrounds, the rich smell of fried food mixed with the sweet smell of cotton candy drifting through the warm air. I walked next to Leo, the two of us trailing a few feet behind the rest of the group. The morning had been filled with jarring carnival rides and noisy games, and now we strolled through the endless pathways of booths and exhibits. Every now and then, the pressing thought of asking Leo to meet my dad entered my mind and I pushed it away, overwhelmed by the sheer humiliation of it. Unfortunately, it was unavoidable. I'd have to ask him at some point. If I didn't bring Leo home to meet my parents, I may as well kiss Jessie's party goodbye, and that was definitely not an option.

"Having fun?" Leo glanced over at me, breaking the brief silence between us.

I forced a smile and nodded reassuringly. "Sorry, I was just thinking about something."

He moved closer, still stepping alongside me, and his arm brushed against mine. I caught my breath at the warmth of his sun-drenched skin. Without a word, he reached out and grabbed my hand. I closed my fingers around his, all of my mind's attention now lost in the strength and smoothness of his palm.

"What is it? What were you thinking about?" he asked. His tone was sweet, as though he were willing to listen to anything I had to say. I hoped it was true. Maybe I could just ask him. Maybe he'd think it was no big deal. I glanced at him again and tried to summon the courage. His dark eyes were settled on my face, waiting patiently.

I took a slow breath. "Well, I wanted to ask—"

"Leo! We're going this way!" Clive called out from up ahead as he turned down a pathway filled with food carts and other tents. "Kai wants to go on more rides!"

Leo flicked his head in agreement and turned toward the path, drawing me along with him. He leaned into me. "Sorry. Tell me what you were going to say."

I shrugged off the interruption and drew in another breath. "Well, it's kind of lame, but I just need to ask you if—"

"Heey Leo!!" a shrill, girly voice called out from behind us.

I whipped my head around at the same time Leo turned. A sudden pang gripped my insides as I took in the sight of Clarissa, the girl from the pool. She was shaking her beach-blonde ringlets out and away from her face as she came toward us. Apparently, the fact that Leo was holding hands with me didn't deter her in the slightest. I felt myself squeezing Leo's fingers, and he tightened his grip around my hand.

With her friend trailing along beside her, Clarissa caught up to us, breathless. "Hey!"

You said that already. I turned pointedly away.

"Hey." Leo made a movement with his head, acknowledging her as little as possible, but if Clarissa was bothered by it she didn't let on.

She smiled as she passed, taking off ahead of us. "We're going on some rides—maybe we'll see you?"

Leo shrugged. He turned back to me. "Wow. I think

she might be psycho." He laughed and squeezed my hand again. "Tell me what you were saying."

I shook my head. "No, it's okay. Later, maybe."

Leo pulled at my arm. "Come on..."

"Not right now." I looked into his face. The sun reflected off his dark hair as the breeze blew wisps of it over his eyes. I wished I could reach up and touch it.

He grabbed at his neck, eyeing me, and I pulled my gaze from his, searching for something else to talk about. In the distance, a round tent flapped in the breeze as we passed by it. Over the doorway a huge banner read:

SHAKESPEARE'S LONDON GLOBE PRESENTS:
A MIDSUMMER NIGHT'S DREAM

"Oh wow! They're doing Shakespeare here," I said, pointing toward the tent. Leo shot me a look as though he wasn't buying the sudden change in subject. I craned my neck to look over at the tent again, intrigued by the red, Renaissance-looking banners. It really would be something great to see.

Up ahead, Jessie made an abrupt stop beside one of the smaller booths. She lifted her arms as if shielding something from view. "Okay, Dove. Do not look to your right. Just move along, nothing to see here."

I laughed, shooting her a fake glare. Behind her, a tent overflowed with old-Hollywood pictures and posters. Black-and-white James Dean and Marilyn Monroe prints were propped beside stacks of other vintage movie star photos. Directly behind Jessie's outstretched hand hung a huge poster of Audrey Hepburn. It was an artsy close-up, revealing only half of her face.

"This one's a classic!" I said, pushing Jessie's arm

away.

Leo stopped alongside me. "You like her? I've seen her before. Who is she?"

"Audrey Hepburn." I smiled at the poster. "And yes. She's amazing."

"Like her?" Jessie rolled her eyes. "She's obsessed with her." She let out a chuckle and headed away to catch up with Kai.

Leo studied the picture. "What's so great about her?"

Audrey's one eye stared back at the two of us as though she were waiting to hear the answer, too.

I bent my head sideways. "I don't even know where to begin—she's just carefree and daring and... confident."

"Oh look!" Kai called out. A few booths away, the group was lingering in front of another small tent with an easel out front. Propped on the easel was a caricature drawing. Kai turned to Jessie as Leo and I joined the group. "This is where we had our picture drawn!"

Inside the tent, an artist sat in front of a second easel. The group clustered around the doorway, watching his hand fly over the paper. A cartoon likeness of the two people posing in front of him started to take shape.

Leo's face lit up as he turned to me. "Let's do it!"

My eyes flew open. "Are you serious?"

He looked at me with a huge grin and nodded, circling the outdoor easel, studying the picture. "It would be fun!" He sounded like a kid almost.

I gazed at him, my expression frozen. This was definitely a side to him I hadn't seen before. It was sweet, really, but we barely knew each other. Wasn't this kind of thing for couples who had been together a while? I looked at the ground awkwardly and then stared out beyond him toward the spinning carnival rides. It was too fast. I shook my head as nicely as possible. "No, c'mon." I pulled his arm forward.

Leo didn't move. His face searched mine for an answer. "Why not?"

For a guy who seemed to be pretty proud of his own coolness, he certainly didn't seem to be worried about it right now. I looked around for Jessie only to find the entire group staring back at me. Isaiah frowned as if to say 'why not?' Jessie just looked confused.

"Maybe next time," I finally said, turning back to Leo.

He shrugged and grabbed my hand again, leading the group away from the tent and toward the carnival area. He didn't say another word to me. My heart sank. I had embarrassed him for sure. Maybe I should have just agreed to it. Why did I have to analyze and second-guess every little thing? I glanced over at him again. His face looked serious, but he was still holding my hand in his—tightly—tighter than before, even. All at once, he stopped in his tracks and turned to me. "Can I talk to you alone?" he asked. His voice was heavy... angry almost.

I nodded at him, unsure where this was going. Maybe publicly humiliating him was enough to make him end our date. I straightened my shoulders, readying myself for anything. *Fine.* If that's what he wanted.

"You guys go ahead. We'll meet up with you in a sec," Leo called out to the group. Over my shoulder, I tried to catch Jessie's attention, but she was deep in conversation with Kai. The two of them kept walking ahead without a glance in my direction.

Pulling me by the hand, Leo stepped off the main walk and led me down a narrow pathway between two small exhibit tents. My mind raced. He really had no right to be angry. And if he was mad, why was he

63

still holding my hand? I hesitated. Just as I decided I might pull my hand away, he stopped and turned to me. His chest rose and fell as he breathed. I glanced away in an attempt to collect myself, and then I faced the discomfort of his serious expression. He didn't move his eyes from mine.

"Well?" I asked, my tone half-curious, half-annoyed. He just stood there, taking me in, his dark hair falling into one eye. I took a tiny step backward. It was difficult to concentrate with his eyes bolted to me like that.

"I couldn't wait any longer." His voice was quiet, intense. He stepped forward and pulled me to him, leaning his face into mine. My breath drew in quickly as he hovered over my mouth, waiting for just a moment before he pressed his lips onto mine. The heat from his skin was dizzying. The seconds ticked by in slow motion as the bright warmth of the sun beat down and distant screams from the carnival rides filled the heavy air. Every movement of his mouth against mine made me want more, and I let myself melt into him, matching his eagerness. Time hung suspended for a moment, until our kissing slowed and he pressed his forehead against mine, smiling.

My eyes searched his face.

"What is it?" he panted.

I tried to hold back a grin. "I thought you were mad at me."

His eyebrows sprang up. "What? Really?" He pressed his hand into my back, pulling me against him as his one eyebrow fell lower than the other. "No, just mad *about* you."

THE METAL RAMP EXIT for the Tilt-a-Whirl banged with every footstep. Jessie and I staggered down it, trailing behind the rest of the group who had stopped and gathered in front of some game booths. I sat down on a nearby bench and Jessie followed, flopping down beside me and laying her head on my shoulder. "I can't take it anymore."

"Me neither," I breathed. "I'm all done."

Jessie sat up, looking toward Leo and Isaiah. Leo had leaned up against one of the booths, and he gestured as he joked about something. Jessie moved closer to me. "So? What happened when you guys disappeared? He totally kissed you, didn't he?"

I pressed my lips together to contain my excitement as I gave a little nod.

Jessie scooted even closer. "Wait till you hear this," she whispered. "Kai ran into Clarissa a little while ago, and Clarissa asked about you and Leo." I glanced over at Leo again as Jessie went on. "Kai said you guys were here together, and then Clarissa told her he wasn't serious about you."

My gut tightened with anger. Or was it embarrassment? I couldn't be sure, but I now despised Clarissa more than ever. And it only added to the upset feeling in my stomach. Leo's kiss had left me on a blissful high, but it couldn't erase the nagging irritation at the thought of still needing to ask him to meet my dad. In fact, it made it worse. I leaned back against the hard bench.

"One more ride?" Leo called out to us, his eyebrows raised.

Jessie and I shook our heads at the same time.

"Noooo," Jessie answered.

"Seriously? No way—sorry," I added with a smile.

Leo let his eyes linger and gave me a knowing look, as if to remind me of our kiss. He turned back to Isaiah as the group circled near the booth along with a few other kids I recognized from school. The noise of the crowd echoed in my ears, and I watched as Leo laughed about something. His smile was perfect, lighting up his whole face, and I suddenly wished we could be alone one more time so I could kiss him again.

At that moment, a blur of white-blonde hair caught my attention in the background beyond Leo. I sat up straight, focusing in. Sure enough, Clarissa was walking toward our group. She stopped inches away from Leo, pretending nothing was up as she chatted with her friend.

I eyed Jessie. "Look who's back."

"Wow. She doesn't give up easy," Jessie sneered.

"Neither do I." I stood and jutted my chin into the air Audrey-style. *Poise. Composure.* My heart began to race, but I strolled over and stopped beside Leo, slipping my hand into his. Out of the corner of my eye, I saw Clarissa shift her weight.

"I changed my mind," I said loudly, so everyone could hear.

An amused smile sprang onto Leo's face. "Okay." He eyed me sideways. "About what?"

"You know." I smiled. "About the cartoon drawing of us. The one you wanted to do earlier?"

"Okay—great!" His face lit up with his dimpled smile.

Isaiah peered at me. "Hold on there—can that wait till I finish telling him my story?"

"Sure, no problem," I said, shrugging. "I'll go sign us up." I pointed toward the artist's tent in the distance and turned to Leo. "Meet me over there?"

His eyes locked onto mine as he nodded. He couldn't have looked more pleased.

Clarissa took a step backward as I brushed past her, catching a glimpse of her glare out of the corner of my eye. With my head held high, I headed off down the wide pathway between the game booths.

In the midst of congratulating myself, something on the ground up ahead gleamed and caught my eye. It looked gold and shiny against the mixture of dirt and sawdust. As I came closer, it looked more and more like a ring or a piece of jewelry.

Just when I bent to grab it, something large thumped into the front of my shoulder, sending me stumbling back. I felt the heavy weight of a person tumbling beside me as I fell backward into the dirt.

"Oh God, I'm so sorry!" a thick English accent called out. I turned to see the owner of the voice: a young guy dressed in a scarlet Renaissance costume, complete with puffed sleeves. He scrambled up and reached out for me. "Are you alright?" he asked in his British way.

"I'm sorry," I said as he helped me up by my arm. "I wasn't looking where I was going." I dusted the dirt from the front of myself.

"No, no, entirely my fault," he returned, tossing his blond hair out of his eyes. His look of concern slowly morphed into a smile. "I'm Henry."

"I'm Dove," I said, still trying to collect myself.

"Dove? Is that really your name?" His accent oozed with charm. "Beautiful."

I blinked at his black tights and boots. "So... are you a part of the Shakespeare Company?"

He grinned. "Either that, or you traveled in time during your fall." His blue eyes danced.

I looked down, scanning the ground. "I was looking

at—that," I said, pointing to a small gold ring at our feet.

He bent over and picked it up. Holding it between his thumb and forefinger, he blew the dirt from it and held it out to me. "Just a bit of plastic, I'm afraid."

My smile was sheepish as I eyed the ring and then pointed at his shirt. "You have sawdust in your... ruffles," I said, unable to come up with a better word for the lace spilling out of his jacket lapels.

He brushed it off, not fazed in the slightest. "So, do you live around here?"

At that moment, I felt the warmth of a hand on my back. Leo leaned into me. "What's up?" He flicked his gaze to Henry and back to me. "You okay?"

"Yes, I fell down, and he helped me up," I said, brushing at my arms again.

"Actually, I knocked you over and then helped you up." Henry smirked.

"It was my fault..." I offered again.

"You ready to do the picture?" Leo asked, turning pointedly away from Henry. He took my hand with a bit more grip than necessary, and the meaning was clear: This is *my* girl, so back off, *Henry*. I bit my lip to keep from grinning. That was one hundred percent genuine jealousy. He was actually jealous over me. I tossed a polite wave to Henry over my shoulder and smiled sideways at Leo as we headed away together.

LEO SAT DOWN IN front of the artist, and I squeezed in next to him. Being on the opposite side of the easel did not come naturally, but I tried my best to suspend my own artistic instincts and surrender to becoming the subject. Leo looked happy as ever, and I glanced sideways at him every now and then, still in minor disbelief at his excitement over something so corny. The rest of the group had joined us at the booth now, watching as the guy behind the easel continued to sketch away. I squirmed in my chair as superficial thoughts floated through my head. Hopefully this guy would make me look pretty. I fidgeted again, now wondering if he would emphasize the roundness of my face too much. Didn't these guys always play up a feature? With any luck, it would be my eyes and not my full cheeks.

The artist set down his large charcoal crayon, lifted his fresh piece of artwork, and turned it to show us.

"It's super cute!" I said, laughing with Leo at our cartoony faces. I took the drawing, holding it up to examine it more closely while everyone crowded around to see. My blonde hair fell in loose curls onto my shoulders, a perfect contrast against Leo's dark hair and the bright carnival colors of the background.

"It looks great!" Kai said, turning to Clive, who managed a smile.

Jessie wedged in to get a better look. "Adorable!"

Isaiah threw in a few humorous comments and I rolled it up, holding it out to Leo.

He shook his head, grinning. "No, I want you to have it," he said, wrapping his arm around me as the group began to walk again. My greasy lunch growled in my stomach. Despite the horrible feeling of time ticking away, I simply couldn't convince myself to bring up the subject of meeting my dad.

As we headed toward the parking lot, Jessie rambled on about the details of her party. I rubbed my forehead. I would have to say it soon.

"The band is amazing, you guys. You're gonna love them!" Jessie announced with a squeal. She turned to me as I stared blankly at the Ferris wheel in the distance, immobilized by what I still hadn't done.

"Dove, what time is it?" Jessie asked, trying to nab my attention.

I broke my trance and looked at my phone. "Four ten."

"We really should get going." Her keys jingled as she pulled them from her purse.

Trotting toward the Jeep, she turned and called out over her shoulder, "Hurry up, we need to get ready!"

"Okay, I'm coming." It couldn't wait any longer. *Just say it.* I turned and faced Leo. "Umm... I need you to meet my dad." I tilted my head, cringing inside at how lame and old-fashioned it sounded. *Don't laugh*, I begged silently.

He gave me a smile, but it was a crooked one. Clearly, he was not accustomed to this subject. "Okay." He wrinkled his forehead, trying to hide his amusement. "When?"

His charming attempt to take it seriously made my cheeks flush with heat. A shy smile crept onto my face, thanking him. "Tonight before the party?"

He looked at the ground and rubbed the back of his head, his hand stopping on his neck. Maybe the reality of it was setting in. His face looked serious, but he grabbed my hand and began to walk me toward Jessie's idling Jeep. "Okay, pick you up at eight?" He stopped beside the Jeep and opened the passenger door, then shut it behind me. I buckled my seatbelt and turned to find him leaning into the open window.

"You're going to leave without kissing me again?" he asked, his eyes sparkling at me.

The last bit of embarrassment melted away. His head moved closer, and I leaned toward him to meet his lips.

"Okay!" Jessie interrupted, putting the car into gear. "Gotta go, lovebirds! You're going to see each other tonight, remember? I'm sure you'll survive till then."

Leo leaned away from the car, his forearms pushing him backward. "See you tonight."

As the Jeep sped away in the warm summer air, I looked down into my lap where the drawing sat, the happy faces of our caricatures staring back at me. At the top of the page, our names were sketched in black charcoal. I leaned my head back and closed my eyes, but the cartoony letters of *LEO and DOVE* still floated in my mind.

Chapter 8

"How do you do?"
-Holly Golightly

Breakfast at Tiffany's

I crawled into my cushioned window seat and looked out at the boats tethered to the docks in the dark harbor. I'd watched the minutes tick away for the last half hour, waiting for Leo to arrive... maybe the bay would distract me. Wind whipped the flags on the rigging of the larger boats, and the water looked choppier than usual. I smoothed my hair in the reflection of the glass, still trying to concentrate on something, anything, outside the window.

The tune of "Moon River" rang out from my phone on my bedside table, startling me, and I smiled at my newest ring tone, reveling in its brilliance. The only thing missing was Audrey's pretty lyrics.

I jumped to answer it. "Hello?"

"Hey," Leo's voice echoed.

"Hey." My heart beat faster.

"I'm almost there, what's the house number?"

"Fifteen forty," I answered. "See you in a sec."

I headed out my bedroom door, pausing for a moment in the doorframe to take in Audrey's serene smile. *Confidence. Poise. Composure.* I repeated silently. Why did it seem so effortless for her and so difficult for me?

I tapped the poster and then shot downstairs, rounding the corner into the kitchen. My dad and Patty were sitting with Griffin at the small table. The casual talking over their dinner plates stopped as they looked up at me.

"Okay, he'll be here in two minutes. Just, you know, be really cool, okay?"

"Baby, I'm always cool." My dad winked.

Griffin smiled, chewing his food. "I'm even cooler."

Confidence. Poise. My internal mantra felt even shakier this time. *Poise. Composure.* No matter how cheerful and supportive my dad tried to sound, I was starting to realize that no one was ever going to be good enough for his only daughter, who he had clearly put on a pedestal. I took a deep breath. That was the thing about pedestals. The person on top of it was trapped. Admired and treasured, but trapped.

The doorbell rang, and I flew toward it as everyone stood, following close behind me. I turned and waved them back, rolling my eyes. Certainly, all four of us didn't need to open the door. I reached out to turn the handle, and the door creaked as it swung toward me.

There he stood, in worn-out jeans and a plaid flannel hoodie, his dark hair and eyes sparkling. The genuine smile on his face was a relief to see, but I detected a hint of shyness in it.

"Leo, hi," I said, opening the door wide enough for him to step into the entryway. My dad and Patty walked forward, smiling.

73

Griffin darted ahead of them. "Hi!"

I let out a nervous laugh. "This is Griffin."

"Hey, buddy." Leo grinned.

"This is my dad, Dr. Courtland," I motioned toward him, "and my stepmom, Mrs. Courtland." The excruciating last-name introduction lingered in the air as awkward as ever, but they all reached out and shook hands.

"Nice to meet you, sir." Leo nodded at my dad and shot his dimpled smile at my stepmom. I glanced at him. *Did he just say 'sir'? What a sweetheart.*

"So, Leo, Dove tells me you play baseball," my dad remarked. An effort at sports talk. This was good.

I studied my dad, willing him to be pleased with Leo. Patty smiled a bit and offered a cordial comment, but I just stood there, half-frozen, mostly not moving my gaze from my dad's face.

And then it happened. He set his jaw and glanced sideways, frowning. There was no mistaking it. I knew perfectly well what that meant. He didn't approve. My insides gripped. *I knew it.* I blinked back the rush of anger. *Not Ivy League enough for you, Dad?*

I had no idea what words were being exchanged now—it was all a blur of sound and movement until Leo and I finally headed out the door and down the brick steps. I shot my dad a serious look, but he just stood there, smiling once again behind a mask of politeness that made me squirm. *Mom would like him!* I wanted to yell at his stiff expression, but I turned away, grabbing Leo's hand as we made our way down the brick path.

I was positive of it. My mom would have loved Leo's laid-back, easygoing way. The fact that his shirt lacked a button-down collar wouldn't have bothered her one bit.

Leo squeezed my knee as we pulled away in his

Bronco. "How'd I do?"

My heart sank. He had braved all that discomfort just for me. There was no way I could tell him what I really thought. "You were perfect. Thank you," I said, my stomach churning at the happy look on his face. I closed my eyes and pushed away my frustration, glad that the three short blocks to Jessie's didn't give me a whole lot of time to think about it.

When we rounded the corner, the street was crowded with parked cars and people milling around in front of Jessie's house. Kids were walking in and out of the side gate, the beat of a bass drum pounding from behind the house. The branches of the huge sycamore tree bent over the fence from where it stood rooted in the backyard, its leaves now pale hues of orange and gold.

Fall was on its way. September had arrived. That meant the official six-year mark of missing my mom would be here soon, too. Just in time to remind me once again how much better everything would be if she were still here.

Chapter 9

"IF YOU LOOKED A LITTLE LONGER, FATHER, YOU'D
FIND HIM RATHER NICE."
-SABRINA FAIRCHILD

Sabrina

Late Sunday morning the kitchen was quiet when I tiptoed in, but the heavy scent of warm butter and melted cheese still lingered from my dad's weekend omelet-making routine. I was glad I had missed it. The party was about as fun as it could have been with his look of disapproval replaying in my mind the whole night. Out of the handful of guys I'd dated, he'd only genuinely liked one of them, and of course that guy had been my least favorite. I knew what to expect. It would all be very subtle and annoying. He'd make it hard for me to date Leo by making me busy all of a sudden with family affairs. My curfew would mysteriously be pushed up under the guise of some kind of school reason, and Leo would probably never be included in any kind of family event.

Hoping to avoid any conversation, I juggled a glass of milk and a box of crackers and headed toward the stairs on my way back to my bedroom.

"Morning, Dove." My dad appeared in the doorway to the family room. "Could you come here for a minute?" he asked, waving me in with his head.

I reluctantly dumped my armload at the bottom of the stairs and stepped into the family room. So much for avoiding any small talk.

He grabbed the remote, muting the news show on the TV. "How was the party?"

His casual, friendly tone grated on me. "Fine." I flopped onto the couch. "It was fun. The band was awesome."

"Well, they were loud enough, that's for sure—we could hear the music from our bedroom." He smiled, but I only nodded. "Good—that's good, Jessie had a nice birthday, then," he said, filling the silence.

I suddenly realized that the stiffness was not coming from just my end. He never talked like this. What was going on? "Is something wrong?" I blurted.

My dad pursed his lips. "Well." He paused. "This week marks the beginning of your senior year, and I'm concerned about the possibility of you losing focus..."

This was way too official sounding. Where was this going?

"Finishing high school and choosing a college should be at the top of the list right now."

"They are." My eyes darted from my dad's face to Patty, who poked her head through the doorway and then stepped into the room, settling herself onto a chair beside my dad.

"So, I've given it some thought, and..." He glanced over at my stepmom.

Yes? The suspense was starting to grip me.

He shifted in his chair and continued. "Well... I

don't really think it's a good idea for you to date anyone right now."

I froze, unable to believe the sentence had left his mouth. I blinked. "What?"

My head started to spin. He'd never taken it this far. Did he really hate the look of Leo that much? He had barely even talked to him. Disjointed thoughts began to bombard my head. Was it the worn-out flannel shirt? Did the old-school Bronco make him seem like some sort of hotshot rebel? I knew my dad could be critical, but this was a whole new level of judgmental.

"This isn't anything personal against Leo," Patty said, emphasizing a cloying, calm tone.

"Yes it is!" I rolled my eyes and shook my head at the floor. Nothing made me miss my mom's relaxed, easy way more than the sound of Patty's fake, forced voice.

She tilted her head in a pleading way. "We just don't want you to get swept away. You're so young—this is not the time in your life to get too serious about anyone."

"Serious about anyone?" I jumped up from the couch. Since when was Patty the concerned expert on dating and relationships? "What are you talking about? We went on a *date*! That's it! I can't believe this…" I looked around the room, searching for an answer. "I just… I don't get it. What about him do you despise so much?"

My dad let out a breath. "Leo is fine."

I scowled.

"I'll admit—he's not exactly the kind of guy I picture you being with long-term…"

Long-term?

"…But this isn't about him."

Yes it is.

"This is about you focusing on what's important right

now. Your future. Your art. And college." He squirmed at the look on my face. "I'm not saying you can't go out and have fun with your friends, but a boyfriend isn't necessary in your life right now."

I couldn't believe this. My mind raced in laps around itself. I took a slow, deep breath and stared, unblinking, at the floor. "So, let me get this entirely straight. You are actually telling me, right here and now, in the twenty-first century, that I cannot date someone I want to date."

My dad wrinkled his forehead. "I didn't want to put it that way, but—yes."

I took a step backward. "That is *crazy*. I'm seventeen years old. *Tell me* what you don't like about him. *Explain* this to me, please, because I am completely lost here."

He just stared at me in silence. He seemed tense... unsure almost.

I rubbed my forehead, trying to take it in. "We'll be seeing each other every day at school, you know. Are you going to try to stop that? What next? Make me move schools?"

Patty shook her head. Was she actually trying to appear sympathetic? "Don't be silly, Dove. You can be friends with him, of course. We just wanted to stop the possibility of any... romance... before it started."

That was it. "Whatever. This is insane." I turned and walked out of the room, unable to reach the bottom of the staircase before the tears finally welled up. Grabbing the railing, I pulled myself upward, determined not to let them see me cry.

Chapter 10

"ISN'T THAT JUST THE WEIRDEST?"
-HOLLY GOLIGHTLY

Breakfast at Tiffany's

I stood in front of my locker, exchanging books and binders from my second to third period class. On the first day of school, Bayport High was always filled with what seemed like more kids than usual. People bumped shoulders trying to navigate through the hallways while everyone shouted and greeted each other after the long summer.

The happy excitement escaped me completely. The night before had been spent agonizing over how to tell Leo how lame my dad and stepmom actually were. Not that I was going to bow to their ridiculous order. If they wanted to be crazy, then I would match it with my own insanity. But my dad was being more than just crazy... he was being plain stupid. Everyone knew what happened when parents tried to control their daughter's every move and treat her like some sort of sequestered princess. It was practically a Hollywood cliché.

Roman Holiday was a case in point. I closed my eyes

and rationalized with myself. It made absolute sense for Audrey to escape her perfect princess world on the back of Gregory Peck's motor scooter—and, well, seeing Leo made complete sense, too. I was seventeen. I could think for myself, and it was time to start listening to my own opinions. Leo and I would see each other whether my dad liked it or not. And if that meant sneaking around, then so be it. He was bringing this on himself.

I grabbed my literature book, trying to focus on my new schedule. *English next—with Leo.* The thought of seeing him and having to actually tell him the news made my stomach twist in a knot. How do you break something like that to someone? *Hey, my dad doesn't like you. Apparently, he doesn't think you're good enough for me, so if you want to go out with me, we'll have to do it in secret.* There was no getting around it. That's exactly what he would think no matter how nicely I tried to word it.

The locker next to mine slammed shut, revealing a girl wearing Doc Marten boots and a long skirt. Her thick, purple bangs fell in a perfect line just above her eyebrows.

"Hey, Greta." I looked over her shoulder, surprised to not find Nate beside her as usual.

"What's up, Dove?" Greta asked in her cheerful way.

"Not much. How's Nate?"

"He's good. How's Leo?" she said without missing a beat.

I frowned. "You know about me and Leo?"

She hooked her big canvas bag onto her shoulder. "Everyone knows about you and Leo, Dove. Seeing all the pictures posted from Jessie's party just cemented the rumors that were flying around." She waved. "See ya."

My eyes followed her as she strolled away, my brain

digesting the words, when the outline of a dark-haired girl came into focus.

I took a breath and found a smile. "Hi, Piper."

She came closer. Her face didn't return the friendly expression. "I cannot believe that *you* are going out with Leo Donovan." She just stood there, glaring.

I blinked at her, not knowing what was more insulting, the fact that she had emphasized the word *you*, or the tone of her voice, which was dripping with disgust. I lifted my chin and looked straight into her eyes to meet her glare. Dang, she was pretty, with her dark hair framing her high cheekbones and pointed nose.

"Thanks, Piper." Sarcasm was always a subtle way to save face without retaliating. Why did she care, anyway? Why was everyone talking about it? I searched for something to change the subject. "How was your trip? You went to Florida, right?"

She narrowed her eyes at me. "He was *my* boyfriend."

I took a small step backward. "What?"

"Oh, don't pretend you didn't know." There was that disgust again. "He's liked me ever since we met over Christmas vacation last year, and we texted when he was in Arizona."

A dizzying sensation made my head reel. I tried to stand a little taller, grasping to stay collected. "Well, I don't know anything about that... and it doesn't sound like he was exactly your boyfriend."

"Oh, really? Would you like to see some of his texts?" She smirked.

My chest pounded. I glanced sideways to see the tall silhouette of Leo walking down the hall toward us. "No," I answered, composing myself. "Let's just ask him."

He continued to walk our way. He wasn't avoiding

us. That was good.

"Fine," Piper snipped.

Fine? My heart raced faster. Piper seemed pretty sure of herself. Common sense said there had to be some truth to it. He was definitely the player type, and Piper was beautiful. If they had met, he would have noticed her.

"Hi," I said, turning to Leo. I paused for a second and then motioned to Piper. "Piper insists that you were her boyfriend, and that I've somehow interfered with that."

Leo raised his eyebrows, and I saw a hint of amusement at my blunt remark. He looked at the floor and then over to Piper. His face fell serious.

Piper just stood there with her arms crossed and her chin jutting into the air. Her cheeks looked red. Was she blushing or just angry? It didn't matter—it only made her look prettier.

"Hey, Piper," he said, his voice calm. "I thought we were kind of casual before. I mean... we haven't talked in a long time."

I looked from him to her and back again. Casual... they were *casual*. Great. So it *was* at least partially true.

"Oh, so you were never my boyfriend?" She uncrossed her arms and looked him up and down.

"No, not really. I mean, maybe last Christmas, if you want to call it that." Leo shifted his weight, eyeing me.

I bit my lip and dropped my gaze to the floor. This just wasn't fair. I knew he had dated a lot of girls, but why did Piper have to be one of them? Piper—my artist archrival—was now standing here claiming dibs on my boyfriend.

People continued to brush past us in the busy hallway as the three of us stared at each other in silence. It was impossible to ignore the fact that Piper looked

83

really hurt, and I hated the sick feeling that now welled up inside. Whatever the circumstances, Piper obviously had feelings for him. Why did he have this effect? Girls just wanted him.

Around us, the hallway began to empty as people made their way into the classrooms. Piper finally turned to me, breaking the quiet. Her eyes narrowed again. "You're a fool, Dove." She threw me one last glare, then tossed her hair over her shoulder and walked away.

Leo winced at me. "I'm sorry, Dove. I liked her for a little while. It was a long time ago. I don't really know what to say. It's over for me."

I moved my gaze down the long hallway. Piper turned the corner without a backward glance. What did she expect me to do? Walk away because she'd staked her claim to him from last Christmas? My thoughts raced. Why did she have to paint me as some kind of boyfriend stealer? The very idea of being accused of breaking the unwritten girl code made me squirm. It wasn't like I'd ever even seen them together. Together. *Great.* He'd made-out with Piper for sure. I looked up at Leo. He just stood there looking serious. My eyes welled with tears and I clenched my jaw, willing them away. So much for finding the right way to tell him about my dad. The moment was ruined. In fact, the whole *day* was ruined.

Closing my eyes, I quietly banged my locker shut. Leo reached out and pulled me to him, squeezing me close. Despite my best efforts at stopping it, a tear dropped onto my cheek, soaking into the soft red fabric of his Angels jersey.

Chapter 11

"It's me that's bothering me."
-Sabrina Fairchild

Sabrina

Tuesday was no better than Monday when it came to breaking the news about my dad to Leo. The look on his face after an argument between his dad and his coach made me rethink my timing, and by the time he finally cheered up a little on Wednesday, I was preoccupied with trying to ignore the official anniversary of my mom being gone. It didn't work though. As usual, sleep had eluded me, I wasn't hungry, and the tears came easier than ever. I saw no reason to add any more anguish to the day by informing Leo of my dad's terrible opinion of him.

After the final bell on Friday, Leo walked with me to Jessie's Jeep on his way to the weight room. I clutched his hand tightly as I weighed whether or not to bring up the subject I had dodged all week. Every time he looked at me with that squint in his eyes, I became more pulled in, more connected and more worried than ever about spilling the bad news. How would he react? Would he even want to deal with it? The longer it dragged on, the more impossible it was to tell him.

We reached the Jeep, and he turned to me, smiling. "Okay, so tonight." His eyes lit up. "The peninsula with everyone, right?"

I nodded, shifting my weight. Now that the weekend had arrived, things were bound to get trickier. Seeing him would require planning and careful tactics. It would be impossible to keep it from him much longer. Jessie shot me a look and started the engine.

"Pick you up?" Leo nodded at me.

"No," I answered quickly.

His grin started to fade, and I quickly forced a smile. "Uh—I'll just ride with Jess and meet you there. That will be easier, don't you think?"

His brow furrowed. "Okay." He hesitated. "You sure you're okay?" I nodded my head. He was clearly referring to missing my mom. Getting through Wednesday had not been easy for me. Little did he know, today my somber mood was all about my dad.

I summoned a reassuring smile. "I'm sure."

He flashed his smile at me and headed away, picking up his pace to join in with a passing group of guys.

Jessie turned the wheel, and the Jeep skidded out of the parking lot. "When are you going to tell him, Dove?"

"I… I tried—" I sputtered.

"Not hard enough." Jessie scowled.

I stared at her for a moment and then moved my gaze out the window.

She shook her head at me. "This is getting ridiculous."

THE FUN ZONE ON the Balboa Peninsula was crawling

with the usual Friday night crowd. The only thing worse than the stuffy air inside the arcade was the loud, electronic dinging of the games ringing in my ears, making it almost impossible to hear what anyone was saying to each other.

A breeze blew in from the back doorway, and I pulled Leo toward it, savoring the fresh air. We stepped into the alley and he gave me his squint. "Too hot?"

"Yes," I said, breathing in the coolness. "Maybe I shouldn't have worn this sweater."

Just like my black ballet flats, the Tiffany-blue crewneck was my version of a classic Audrey fashion basic—my go-to whenever I was in a hurry or at a loss for what to wear.

He reached out for my hand, pulling me closer. "I love this sweater. It matches your eyes perfectly. You were wearing it that first night at Jessie's—remember?" He squeezed me, teasing me with his smile. "When you completely ignored me?"

I studied him as I laughed. He seemed so relaxed and at ease. Maybe now would be a good time to tell him.

At that moment, two girls walked past. Their eyes darted from Leo to me to our clasped hands. Leo glanced at them before he looked away, and I wondered if his gaze had lingered a little too long. A heat burned in my chest. Girls had been paying him a lot of attention all night. Was it more than usual? Or was I only noticing it more now? I checked myself. Jealousy. Possessiveness. These were both new to me. I pushed the girls out of my mind, trying to rise above it. Maybe it just came with the territory.

Behind us, Clive popped his head outside. "We're going over to the pier," he said as the rest of the group

87

pushed through the back doorway.

Leo and I fell in behind everyone as we made our way across the street to the ocean side of the peninsula. Straight ahead, the Balboa Pier stretched out into the ocean above its huge pylons. In the darkness, the lights from Ruby's Diner sparkled out in the distance at the very end. I gazed off to the right and left. The peninsula beach was so different from the rocky, coved beaches of Corona del Mar and Laguna. Here, long stretches of flat, sandy shore extended out far in both directions.

Heading the group, Isaiah and Clive turned off the boardwalk and onto the beach toward the nearest lifeguard stand. A bunch of kids had grouped around it, talking and laughing in the dark. I slipped off my shoes, loving the soft, cold feeling of the sand.

"Leo!" one of the guys in the circle called out.

Leo stepped over next to him, and I turned to talk with Jessie near a group of girls who had clustered together.

"Did you tell him?" Jessie looked hopeful.

"No." I hated saying it.

"Why not?" Jessie's tone was softer.

"I don't know."

"Just do it, Dove." She shook her head at me. "He'll be cool about it."

I scowled.

"He really likes you. I don't think he's going to let anything stand in his way. And if he doesn't like it, then forget him." She frowned at me. "This isn't like you—since when are you so worried about some guy's approval?"

Since I completely fell for him. I looked down at the dark sand, cursing myself for getting to this point. "You're right."

Jessie nodded urgently, her eyes wide, as though to encourage me along.

"Yes," I declared, gearing myself up.

She squeezed my hand and stepped in toward Kai and the other girls, leaving me to ponder that last thought. Standing at the edge of the circle, I tuned out the chatter of the girls and looked over at Leo in the midst of all the guys. I strained my ears, focusing in on their conversation.

"Trina?" a tall guy said. "Yeah, I used to date her."

A bunch of laughter muffled someone's response. Leo just stood there, listening.

"You went out with her, didn't you, Isaiah?" another guy asked.

Isaiah shook his head. "No, Leo did though."

The guys all looked at Leo. He gave them a nonchalant smile.

My stomach flipped. *Trina who?* Great. They were talking about ex-girlfriends.

Clive looked up at the blue-painted wood of the lifeguard stand, checking out the large black letter *M* painted on the side. "Tower M. I'm pretty sure I worked this one."

"You were a lifeguard?" one of them asked.

"Yeah, last summer," Clive answered.

The tall guy walked over and slapped one of the wooden posts. "I was never a lifeguard, but I'm pretty sure I worked this stand, too."

A loud burst of laughter erupted from all of them.

Worked it? Okay, wow. I rolled my eyes to myself. There had always been rumors of people doing it inside lifeguard towers late at night, but I was never sure if they were true. This blew the lid off that one.

More of their muffled talk floated across the sand

toward me. "I know who else worked it," another guy called out. "Leo did for sure, didn't you, Leo?"

I felt myself stop breathing.

Leo leaned against the lifeguard stand with no idea I was staring, taking in the whole conversation. He dipped his head sideways and let out a reluctant laugh. "Yeah, I worked it."

I froze. I wasn't sure what bothered me more... the fact that he had slept with a girl right here on this beach, or the fact that he was bragging about it now, only twenty feet away from me.

My heart raced. He was joking about his conquests while here I was agonizing over breaking the news about my dad not even allowing me to *date* him. What was wrong with this picture? I watched as he threw his head back, laughing with the guys. All of a sudden, he seemed like a complete jerk.

My hands shook as I smoothed my hair in an effort to find some semblance of calm. I looked in his direction again, and a wave of energy rippled through me at the sight of the moonlight reflecting off his dark hair. I clenched my jaw at myself. When had he wormed his way this far into my heart? The complexity of it all was overwhelming. Maybe it was time to just say forget it and walk away before this need I felt for him grew any bigger or stronger. Besides, with all these girls throwing themselves at him all the time, why would he even want to deal with me and my parental problems anyway? My heart pounded faster. More than anything at that moment I needed to get away from him, to be alone. But how?

I looked over my shoulder at the tree-lined street leading back over to the bay side of the peninsula. It would be easy to just take the ferryboat to Balboa Island

and walk home across the bridge. With so many people around, no one would notice for at least long enough to make it over to the ferry landing. I could text Jessie when I was safely aboard.

With my heart beating against my ribs, I took a step backward and slid my gaze back to Leo. He was still talking with the guys. A swarm of people walked past, and I seized the opportunity to blend in with their group. Skirting around them, I picked up my pace down the short street, glancing over my shoulder only once before I darted across the crosswalk still in my bare feet, my flats dangling from my fingers.

Chaotic dinging and ringing filled my ears again as I slipped on my shoes as fast as possible and passed by the arcade along the bay front, trying my hardest to fight away the guilt. It was better this way. If I'd said goodbye he would have argued and pleaded, and my head wasn't clear enough for that right now. All I knew was that being with Leo was turning out to be way too difficult and painful. I picked up my already fast pace. The best decision was to end it... and maybe making him angry by disappearing would just make it that much easier.

"Dove!" Leo's voice shouted out from behind me.

I jumped at the sound of it. Without looking, I started to run.

"Dove, wait!"

I ran even faster down the sidewalk, weaving my way between couples strolling hand-in-hand and a few kids munching on corn dogs. I could see the ferry up ahead. The third and final car loaded onto it while the pedestrians and bicyclists had already been seated. It was about to leave. *Hurry.* With the sound of Leo's footsteps growing closer, I dashed down the ramp as the large metal railing lowered and the ferry's horn blew.

"Wait!" I called out to the attendant perched on the ferry's edge. The small ferryboat pulled away from the landing, and I stopped abruptly at the end of the dock, panting.

"Sorry," the guy called out. "Next one's right there." He pointed out to another ferry floating just off the docks, waiting for its turn to unload.

I winced at the sound of Leo's footsteps now pounding on the dock behind me. Bracing myself, I turned to face him.

"What are you doing?" he breathed. "Where are you going?" He stopped in front of me, panting and scowling in confusion.

I steeled myself. "I'm going home."

His face morphed into wounded. "What the hell, Dove? That's all you have to say?"

My hands started to shake. I wanted to reach out and pull him to me—tell him I was sorry, but I pushed away the impulse. "I just... I need to go home, Leo, and I'll explain it all to you tomorrow or something." What was I saying? I was making no sense. I sounded like some sort of cryptic, crazy person.

Guilt sprang into my chest at his shocked expression. He looked like he was grasping to stay calm. "I have no idea what the hell you are talking about, Dove. But at least let me drive you home."

I shook my head. *Precisely the problem.* "You can't." The tension inside me was ready to burst.

"Why not?" he frowned.

"Because my dad told me I can't go out with you!" I blurted.

His face twisted. "What?"

"He... doesn't want me to see you." Tears welled when I said it, but I clenched my fists, commanding them not to come.

"When did this happen?"

"Right after Jessie's party." I bit my lip to keep the tears back.

"Why didn't you tell me?" His face was hard, angry.

"I wanted to... I tried, but..." I could feel every part of myself put up its defenses. Here's where I would suddenly become less desirable to him than before, and I wasn't about to give him the satisfaction of wanting him more than he wanted me. There were plenty of girls waiting in the wings who fit that bill, and I wasn't going to be one of them. Maybe he could give Trina or the lifeguard-stand girl a call for that matter.

Leo just stood there scowling, while behind us the next ferry bumped up against the dock. The railing lifted, allowing the passenger cars to drive up the ramp and onto the peninsula. A few people unloaded from the side, walking their bicycles between the two of us as we stared at each other in silence.

He let out an angry half-laugh. "So, this is it?" His eyes searched mine.

"I guess so." I shrugged, forcing myself to look past him at the lights in the distance.

He shook his head at me, his face twisting again. "Then why did you even come here tonight?"

I squared my shoulders, trying my best to be sensible and mature, or at least come across that way. *Poise. Composure.* "I thought... I thought maybe we could find a way to make it work, but now I realize I was wrong."

Behind me, the ferry had now reloaded with the cars headed to Balboa Island. The railing was about to close. I clenched my jaw, holding in the tears. "I'm sorry, Leo." I said it as firmly and nicely as possible, turned away from him, and stepped aboard just as the railing started to lower.

The horn blew as the ferry pushed away from the dock. I kneeled onto the wooden bench and leaned out over the water. The night breeze blew through my hair, cooling the hotness in my cheeks as the ferryboat continued to cut through the darkness of the bay. I closed my eyes. *It's better this way.* After waiting for what felt like an eternity, I forced myself to turn, looking behind me toward the dock in the distance. Leo was gone.

Chapter 12

"Suddenly you're afraid and you don't know what you're afraid of... do you ever get that feeling?"
-Holly Golightly

Breakfast at Tiffany's

The walk along the seawall of Balboa Island to its main street was longer than I remembered. It'd been several summers since I biked this route to the peninsula with my middle school friends, feeling so independent. The night air was colder now, and the thin fabric of my blue sweater was no match for it. I crossed my arms for warmth as I finally turned onto Marine Avenue, walking past the crowded, noisy cafés and darkened, closed storefronts of the boutiques.

I took a deep breath and exhaled slowly, fighting the idea that maybe I'd been unfair. It didn't matter. Life wasn't fair. And the whole point anyway was to just stop the madness that had begun when I'd met Leo. Drastic times called for drastic measures. I passed underneath the giant frozen banana sign above the Sugar 'n' Spice ice cream stand, weaving my way past the crowd of people lined up outside the customer window. I didn't bother to look over—I knew that window by heart. Just inside it, little containers of nuts and candy sprinkles were lined up, ready for the dipping of a frozen banana or an ice cream bar covered in melted chocolate. My mom had taught me well—Balboa Bars were hands-down the best dessert ever invented. The dripping, chocolate mess had always been our favorite thing to eat on a hot summer day.

A horn honked from the street, and I looked over my shoulder. My stomach lurched at the sight of Leo's blue Bronco rolling along beside me. I shot my gaze forward again, picking up my pace. *Unbelievable.* Apparently, he didn't know the definition of goodbye.

"Let me drive you home, Dove. It's getting late," he called out.

I continued to look straight ahead. "No thanks. I'm a big girl, you know."

I let myself glance over at him. He moved his gaze from me to the street in front of him and back again as he guided his car along. "You look freezing cold—please?" he shouted.

"No. I'm fine, thank you. And you're forgetting one of the main points here. You can't drive me home because my parents will see you, remember?"

He pulled the truck into an empty spot next to the curb beside me. "Whatever, Dove. I'll drop you off a block away, then. It's not that hard."

I passed right by him, striding along as the sidewalk began to slope upward over the two-lane bridge. Leo steered the Bronco onto the street once more and rolled up alongside me again, the engine idling quietly. "Dove, please get in the car."

"Go away, Leo," I said without looking at him.

"Damn it, Dove. You're so stubborn."

I dipped my head sideways, acknowledging it. "Yes, I've heard that before."

A loud honk blared from a car behind him. "Go around!" Leo shouted at it, his voice hard. He turned to me again. "This is crazy, Dove."

I continued to hurry along in silence. Leo matched my quiet for a moment and then finally spoke. "Yeah." He paused a long moment. "I can see why you like her so much."

I spun my head in his direction. "Who?"

"That movie star—Audrey Hepburn. You said she was… what? Carefree? And daring?"

My heart beat faster and I tried to ignore him as I kept walking. What was he getting at?

He continued on in his casual tone, "You know what I think? I think that's the kind of person you really are, but you're just too afraid to be that way."

My breath caught. I was definitely not expecting that one. How dare he. My nostrils flared as I blinked his words away. His evaluation felt a little too close for comfort, but I forced out a scoff. "This, from the rebel without a cause. Please spare me the psychobabble."

"What is that supposed to mean?" Two cars behind him made their way into the opposite, oncoming lane on the bridge, swerving their way around the Bronco.

"It means you should analyze yourself and your need to get laid in lifeguard stands before you point any fingers at me."

Leo fell silent for a moment. "Oh." He was quiet again. "*That's* what this is about? That was… just guy talk."

"Whatever," I said, rolling my eyes.

"Okay, Dove. You're right." He paused. "I'm really

sorry. I am. I shouldn't have said it... but *you* should have told me about your dad."

His voice was steady. I began to feel my resolve weaken. He was right. And here he was, trying so hard to be levelheaded and reasonable about it all. More and more I wanted to stop walking, but my heart pounded in confusion, and the hurt and frustration kept my feet moving.

Another car now followed closely, its headlights shining behind us. Leo ignored it, continuing to roll the Bronco along slowly over the top of the bridge. "I'm gonna say something else, too." He let the statement linger for a few seconds in the air. "I think you're scared of how you feel about me."

I stopped and turned to him. The Bronco stopped, too, and Leo's eyes locked onto mine. My chest rose and fell with my breath, his words still echoing in my head. The silence between us grew heavier as each second ticked by, but his dark eyes didn't waver as he waited.

The car behind us honked long and loud. Leo turned his head. "Go around!" he shouted. The driver leaned on the horn again as the car swerved and passed. In the distance, more headlights approached in a line behind us.

"You can't just keep blocking everyone." I shook my head at him, ignoring the real issue.

His forehead wrinkled as he begged with his eyes. "*Please*," his voice was soft, measured. "Please get in the car so we can talk?"

Several short honks came from the row of cars now stopped behind us. I glanced up into the starless sky to search for an answer and then met his eyes again. Without a word, I opened the car door and slid into the passenger seat.

Leo's dad's condominium sat close to the beach near the base of the peninsula. As the Bronco turned into the complex, I considered the irony of the fact that we had now circled almost all of Newport to end up on the peninsula again.

Leo parked near a short stairway leading up to the front door of the condo, and together we climbed the steps in silence. He swung open the door, and we walked inside the dimly lit entry. A set of stairs rose to a second level above the entryway, and off to the right I could see the kitchen down the hallway. As Leo closed the front door, a tall man appeared in the kitchen doorframe.

"Oh—hey, Dad." Leo seemed surprised.

His dad nodded his head. His hair was dark like Leo's, but with gray streaked around his temples.

"This is Dove," Leo said.

His dad nodded again, his face somewhat friendly but only half-interested. "Nice to meet you, Dove."

He disappeared into the kitchen, and Leo led me into the living room. "Sorry, I thought he was gone... we'll be alone in here."

I sat down on the sofa and blinked at the coffee table, trying to gather my thoughts. I wasn't even sure what to think anymore. The roller coaster of emotions had left my head feeling fuzzy, and Leo's examining looks weren't helping matters much. I had no idea where to go from here.

He sat down beside me, but I didn't move my stare from the shiny glass of the table.

"Dove." He waited until I looked at him. "I'm really sorry." He was so steady, so sure of himself.

"Me too," I offered.

"You okay?" His deep look of concern made my face flush with warmth. I nodded, smiling to reassure him.

"Do you think maybe... some of this is about your mom, too?" He hesitated again before continuing. "It's just... you didn't talk much the other day."

The way he tiptoed around me with his careful tone made my heart swim with a wave of gut-wrenching grief mixed with love for his understanding. He'd hit on the truth yet again. Why hadn't I recognized that myself?

He moved closer, bending his head to mine. "I'm so sorry. Everything will be okay. I just want to be with you..."

I shook my head, stopping his words. "It's just... it's not that simple, Leo."

He winced at me and leaned in. "Yes, it is—that's what I'm trying to tell you." He grabbed my hand and stared at it for a moment. "Let's cut through all the crap. I have a past, and I can't change it," he said, looking up at me. "You have a controlling dad, and you can't change that. All I know is, I want to be with you... I *have* to be with you, because..." He paused, breathing as he searched my eyes with his. "I love you."

I felt my eyes widen as my heart began to pound against my ribcage. Everything in the room fell away, leaving only his eyes staring into mine. Had he really just said that?

Leo laughed at the shocked look on my face, shrugging it away. "It's true. Call me crazy, but I'm completely in love with you." He squeezed my hand, his gaze still locked onto my wide eyes. "And I think you love me."

Warmth rushed over me at hearing the words spoken. It was so simple. He knew it. I knew it. And now hearing it said out loud was like finally owning it. I drew in a breath, taking it in. Somehow it was a relief to embrace the scary, wonderful truth.

He leaned in closer. "And if that's true, then we should be together. *Nothing* should keep us apart."

My eyes searched his face, in awe at his ability to just say what he felt. "You're right." I leaned toward him, gathering my courage. "I do love you, Leo." The captivated look on his face made me even braver. "And I want to be with you."

He bent toward me and brushed his lips against my mouth, his eyes still open, staring into mine. I didn't let my eyes close, locking my gaze with his as our lips moved in gentle touches, our mouths and our eyes communicating, binding us together without words. He stopped and pulled me closer, his gaze roving over my face, scanning every inch of it, loving every bit of me.

I let the moment wash over me, wanting to freeze this feeling forever, this feeling of being present and connected—connected to myself, to him, to life. I held my gaze steady on his face, not daring to move, hoping the magic would linger for a second more.

"Dove." He looked like he was concentrating. "Perfect name for you. Your dad may be slightly whacked, but he got your name right."

I let out a laugh. "Actually, it was my mom's idea."

"No wonder." He locked eyes with me. "Really... you're like a bird," he insisted. "You seem delicate on the outside, but underneath that you're strong and... able to fly."

I tilted my head back so my eyes could wander his face, drinking in his intense stare.

"Yep, like a bird." He squinted his smile at me. "That's what I'm going to call you from now on... Birdy."

Chapter 13

"MR. BRADLEY'S JUST BEEN TELLING ME ALL ABOUT
HIS WORK."
-PRINCESS ANN

Roman Holiday

Bundled in my navy coat, I sat in my usual spot at the edge of the dock, mindlessly sketching the gray October sky that stretched out above the tops of the homes across the bay. My thoughts wandered to Leo as they always seemed to do, and I began to draw the outline of his face inside one of the billowing clouds. It hadn't been easy, but we'd managed to pull off being together for the last month and a half without my dad suspecting a thing. I gripped my pencil tightly at the thought but refused to let it bother me, consoling myself instead with the idea of what my mom's opinion would have been. After all, if there had been one theme to all the vintage movies we saw together, it had to be love. Maybe in some conscious or unconscious way she had been trying to show me something about life. Maybe she wanted me to believe in love. I drew in a breath as I concentrated on sketching the curve of Leo's mouth.

Even I had to admit that my love theory was a bit of a stretch. But it was something to hold onto, at least. One thing I knew for sure, my mom had always told me to stand up for what I believed in and fight for what was right. And these feelings I had for Leo were definitely worth fighting for.

Even so, the craziness of life itself, mixed with everything else, had made it more than challenging to see Leo outside of the time we spent together at school. Homework was enough to keep me home for at least half the weekend, which actually worked out okay, I had to admit, since there were only so many times I could go out with Leo under the guise of being with Jessie. I winced at the thought of it. I seemed to always be worrying now about not wanting to overburden my best friend, who had been covering for me repeatedly.

On top of everything, the looming necessity of finishing college applications had my dad in stressed-out mode, which only intensified my own unease about it all. Tackling the huge chore had been overwhelming, but what really had me on edge was figuring out where I might actually end up. And that brought the issue around to Leo again.

I sketched a bit of dark hair falling over his eyes. Leo. Letting a guy influence my choice of colleges was something I never thought I'd do. But I never thought I'd fall for someone my senior year, either. Now everything had changed. And Leo's future plans at least deserved consideration. He was on track to be drafted into the major leagues right after graduation. A scout from the San Francisco Giants had shown interest in him for the past year, and I couldn't help believing that it might be some sort of serendipity. The San Francisco Art Institute had already been on my radar, but now, ironically, Patty's choice of a college for me had moved to the top of my list.

I pushed away the doubts that sprang up. After all, it wasn't like Leo and I would even be together all the time. Most likely he'd play for the team's minor league in Fresno for the first few years. But we'd be a lot closer to each other than if I were halfway across the country, or in Europe.

Europe—that was another thing. My aunt had insisted that I send the scholarship application for Parsons at the beginning of September. But between my dad's opposition to the whole thing and Leo now in the picture, I had decided to let the whole idea go. Timing was everything. Someday I would get to Paris, and when I did my mom would watch from above as my inner Audrey Hepburn and I strolled along the Seine. But for now, I wasn't going to push it, and with the art gallery money I had been saving for Paris I could build up for a down payment on my own car.

"Dove!" Griffin popped his head out between the sliding French doors. "Dinner!"

Folding the pages over on the sketchpad, I made sure to cover the drawing of Leo's face before I buried it in the storage box and headed up the dock. I gathered my thoughts, readying myself for the usual college-applications-Sunday-dinner discussion, and sat down at the table. Time to sell my dad on the possibility of San Francisco.

My stepmom was the last to join the table, scooting in her chair. "How's it going with applications?"

Somehow, I stifled the smug looked that popped onto my face. The subject really was like clockwork. Except this time, Patty hadn't even waited until the first bite was taken. "Great. Yes... I'm almost finished."

"Just let me know if you need any help, then." Her plastered bun didn't move as she nodded, taking a huge bite of the salad piled on her plate.

Just as I opened my mouth to comment, my dad cut in. "You know, we really should take a trip to Chicago pretty soon here to check out the School of the Art Institute."

I eyed my dad, my wheels turning. *Tread carefully*, I told myself. Chicago was his hometown. He lived and breathed the Cubs, the Bulls, and the Bears. In his mind, Chicago walked on water, and it was the only place I belonged. He'd even gone so far as to send me out to the Art Institute for their summer program my sophomore year.

"Well..." I tilted my head. "I don't really think I need to see it again, Dad. I already got a good feel for it."

"You're older now—you may enjoy it in a different way. And we could make a family trip of it, you know, visit Grandma while we're there," he said, taking a sip of his wine.

"That sounds fun!" Griffin said with his mouth full.

I watched the hand move on the grandfather clock, preparing myself to say it. "Actually, I was thinking I might like to visit the San Francisco Art Institute."

My dad stopped chewing. "Really?"

I gave him a nonchalant shrug and nodded.

"I think it sounds like a great idea, Rick," my stepmom chimed in, as excited as ever. "Don't sound so surprised. You knew she might apply there."

He cleared his throat. "Apply there—yes."

"Well, if she's applying, she's interested." My stepmom let out a clipped laugh.

Yes. Patty to the rescue.

"Where else besides those two?" My dad's obvious

attempt to sound open-minded didn't fool me as he wiped his mouth with his napkin.

"Let's see, I think we've narrowed it to Savannah College of Art and Design—and Parsons, Paris," I added, flicking my gaze at him. "Aunt Gail insisted."

Griffin piped up again. "Can I have more milk?"

I seized the opportunity to escape. "I'll get it for you." Grabbing hold of his glass, I headed through the swinging door to the kitchen, straining my ears to make out my dad and Patty's hushed tones.

The refrigerator door swung closed, and with a full glass of milk I turned toward the dining room. At that moment, the musical sound of "Moon River" began to ring out. My heart jumped. *My phone.* I'd left it on the dining table. I cursed myself as I leapt into a run, scrambling toward the door. That was now Leo's ring. And *only* Leo's ring. I'd programmed the song just for his phone number.

Milk splashed onto the floor as I pushed through the door to the dining room, the music still carrying on from my phone, which was now in Griffin's hand.

"No, Griffy! I'll get it..." I called out, trying my best not to sound desperate. It was too late. Griffin put the phone to his ear. "Hello?"

My heart hammered as I set the glass of milk down, eyeing my dad stiffly.

"Yes, this is Griffin. Who's this?"

Don't say it. He wouldn't say who he was; I tried to convince myself. He would know better. I stood over Griffin, wanting more than anything to grab the phone out of his hand. My dad had stopped talking, now watching what was happening, waiting to see who had called.

Oh. Crap. My heart pounded in full force now as I

stood there, frozen, waiting.

Griffin held the phone out to me. "It's Joe Bradley."

I coughed at the name, almost choking on air. Joe Bradley? There was only one Joe Bradley I knew of... I knew him quite well, actually. Only, he wasn't a real person. He was Gregory Peck's character in *Roman Holiday*. My thoughts raced. How would Leo ever know that name?

My gaze flicked over to my dad. I searched for any signs of doubt as I reached for the phone, but he just started in on his dinner again, eating alongside Patty in silence.

I held the phone to my ear. "Hello... Joe."

Leo's quiet laugh sounded on the other end. "Hey. What do you think of the fake name?"

I sat down in my chair, carefully guarding my reaction. "Good," I said, making the word lilt as though Joe had asked how I was doing.

"I watched *Roman Holiday* today. Figured I should see what the big deal was about her."

"Really?" Whether he knew it or not, he had just scored huge points. "What did you think?"

"She's pretty cool." He paused. "I like you better."

A big smile wanted to escape, but I held it in. "So actually, can I call you back? We're having dinner right now."

Leo laughed out a short goodbye, and I shoved the phone safely into my back pocket this time before picking up my fork.

"So, who's Joe Bradley?" Patty asked, passing a plate of potatoes to Griffin.

A guilty smirk emerged at the absurdity of her question. I bit it back. "He's just a friend."

"Someone from art class?" She looked like the

picture of unsuspecting curiosity.

As I finished my mouthful, I pictured Gregory Peck carting Audrey all over Rome as he scribbled notes for his newspaper story onto his notepad. "No. I think he's into journalism."

Chapter 14

"Gelato? Thank you!"
-Princess Ann

Roman Holiday

"*Ciao artista!*" Angelo's deep voice called out. I stepped through the jingling café door and greeted him with a smile before I looked toward the window seats. All of the tables in the restaurant were filled with people talking over their lunches.

"He's over here!" Angelo said, pointing to a table near the coffee counter.

My eyes landed on Leo, who was sitting in a booth, smiling at me. I slid onto the cushioned seat opposite him, and he grabbed my hand, wrapping my fingers in his. "Hey, Birdy."

I gave a quick smirk at the nickname I couldn't get used to. There was something incredibly sweet about it, though.

Angelo stepped alongside us, his white apron stretched across his large belly. "I'm sorry I don't have a window seat for you today," he said, handing us each a menu. "The holiday crowd is keeping me busy... Ah!"

He pointed his finger in the air. "I have a special gelato for you today. You must try it after lunch!" he exclaimed, raising his bushy eyebrows.

Angelo moved to the next table, and Leo leaned in. "There's no doubt about it," he whispered as he looked over his shoulder at Angelo, then back to me, raising one eyebrow. "He's the *Lady and the Tramp* guy." His eyes sparkled as he squeezed my hand.

"You could be right." I faked a serious shrug, drinking in the sight of him. His dark hair was pushed back from his eyes, which were fixed on me. "Missed you," I said, leaning closer.

School was out for Thanksgiving, and with Jessie gone to her grandparents' for the long weekend it had been more difficult than ever to find ways to get together. My Saturday lunch break was our first and only opportunity, and thankfully Aunt Gail understood about such things. "I can't actually *help* you two, but I'll look the other way," she'd said with a wink.

I never thought I'd dislike having days off from school, but if a few days of vacation were as frustrating as this, then I didn't even want to think about how hard Christmas break was going to be.

"Think you can get away tonight?" he asked with a frown. "My dad just left for a last-minute trip to New York. Everybody's coming over to hang out."

I looked sideways, examining the idea. "I don't think I can do it. Not without Jessie here to cover for me."

He glanced at the table, flashing a look of disappointment.

"Any more news from the Giants?" I said, searching for something cheerful.

"Yeah, actually. The scout was at batting practice again the other day talking to the coach, and then my dad showed up, of course." He tilted his head back and let out a scoff. "Seems like the only time he ever gives a crap about me is when I'm playing baseball."

I anchored my stare on him, knowing better than to try to fix it with words. He didn't talk about his dad much, but when he did it was never pleasant.

"It's okay. It's always been like that." He shrugged away my look of concern. "Anyway, my mom's awesome, though."

I studied him. "How is your mom? I can't wait to meet her."

"She's good. She wants to see me over Christmas."

"Great!" I gave him an encouraging nod. "So she's coming to visit?"

"No... I'm going to go see her." He winced.

Disappointment washed over me. All of a sudden, searching to find ways to be together didn't sound half as bad as him not even being in town. "Oh."

Angelo appeared beside our table, his small notepad in hand. He flipped the top page over, smoothing it. "Have the lovebirds decided?"

I flicked a glance at Leo and bit back my smile. Leo held in a laugh, scanning his menu. As I lifted my head to give my order, the front door behind Angelo jingled as it opened. A man's silvery-white hair glinted in the sun as he walked in beside a woman dressed in hot pink yoga pants, her hair pulled tightly into a blonde bun. I was dumbstruck. For a split second, my eyes froze in round circles.

My dad and Patty.

Without another glance at Leo or Angelo, I ducked my head and quickly slid underneath the table. My heart began to race as thoughts flew through my mind. Why would they come here on a random Saturday? They never came here by themselves—only with me after work, sometimes. What were they doing here?

From my new, floor-level viewpoint, I could see only legs and feet. Leo's were right beside me, unmoving. Angelo's big, black shoes were walking toward the door where my parents now stood.

"Ah, it's the Courtlands! How nice to see you!" he bellowed in his thick, Italian way. "Have you seen your daughter's latest masterpiece?" He held his arms out and turned them toward the wall, where two paintings hung between the windows. All of their feet pivoted and walked toward my painting of the Balboa Ferry, which was now displayed, as Angelo had insisted, next to my other piece.

I got it. *Brilliant.* Angelo was distracting them on purpose. This was my chance. I scooted forward underneath the edge of the table and then hesitated. The front door was only a few feet away from Patty— dangerously close. There was no way I could make it out that way. In the other direction, behind the coffee counter, the door to the kitchen still swung on its hinges from a bus boy pushing through. I crept forward an inch more and looked over at my dad and Patty again. If I stood, one of them might catch sight of me out of the corner of their eye. I couldn't risk it. As fast as possible, I began to crawl on my hands and knees toward the rounded end of the coffee counter.

Scrambling along the wood floor, I ventured a backward glance. Leo was successfully burying himself in his menu. At a table just beyond him, a woman was staring at me, her fork stopped halfway to her mouth. Over by the windows, Angelo gave a quick look over his shoulder. His eyes bulged momentarily before he turned back, talking louder than ever in order to keep my parents' attention. I finally reached the end of the counter and crawled behind it. Hopping onto my feet, I ducked my way over to the kitchen door and quickly pushed through.

The kitchen was noisy with the sound of dishes and pans clanking, but the handful of guys dressed in white restaurant aprons carried on with only a glance or two in my direction. I leaned against a metal rack filled with plates, trying to catch my breath. The thumping in my chest began to slow. I made it.

Angelo bumped his way through the kitchen door, holding two dirty plates. He shook his head at me as he set the dishes into the sink. "I hope you know what you are doing, *artista*."

I tried not to look sheepish. "I'm so sorry. Thank you, Angelo."

He wiped his hands on a dishcloth. "*Amore*," he said with a slow shake of his head. "It makes us do crazy things."

My back pocket buzzed, and I grabbed my phone. *I'm out. Meet me in back.*

"That's him." I looked up at Angelo, who now smiled. "Thank you again, Angelo. You saved my life."

He winked at me before leading me to the back door, and then swung it open to the alley. I stepped into the sunlight to the sight of Leo waiting for me, his hands in his jacket pockets.

"Wait, wait!" Angelo held both hands up to us and then quickly disappeared inside.

I moved toward Leo, who was now both grinning and shaking his head at me.

"What? Did I look ridiculous?" I bit my cheek, frowning at him.

He just laughed and put his arms around me,

pulling me close. "Nah, you did great."

I laid my head against his chest. "I'm so sorry. I wish we didn't have to deal with this."

His chest rose and fell with a deep breath, and he squeezed me tightly. I felt the warmth of his breath against my ear as he whispered, "It's worth it."

"For the lovebirds!" Angelo called out. Leo and I turned to see Angelo in the doorway holding two huge waffle cones filled with scoops of pink gelato. "*Fragola!*" he shouted. "Strawberry!"

"Thanks, Angelo!" I said as we stepped toward him.

He handed one to each of us. "The fruit of love… it's perfect for you, no?" he asked, his accent thicker than ever.

Leo and I exchanged looks, smiling as Angelo grabbed the doorknob and leaned toward us with a wink. "And today—it's on the house!" he said, swinging the door shut.

Leo blinked and then lowered his eyelids at me. "You do realize we are in the alley behind his Italian restaurant, and he just gave us food and talked about love, right?"

I took a bite of my ice cream, chuckling as I shook my head at him.

"Yep." He faked a serious nod. "*Lady and the Tramp* guy. Exactly what I've been trying to tell you all along." He gave me an exaggerated shrug. "Now do you believe me?"

Chapter 15

"I SUPPOSE YOU THINK I'M VERY BRAZEN OR TRÈS
FOU, OR SOMETHING."
-HOLLY GOLIGHTLY

Breakfast at Tiffany's

December brought a chill to the air—significant for Southern California at least, and enough to force everyone out of flip-flops and into their sheepskin boots.

I was quiet as I lay on top of Jessie's bed, staring up at the heating vent blowing warm air at me. Jessie sat on the floor, buried in pages of notes, with open textbooks spread all around. I rolled over, picked up the pen lying on the notebook beside me, and clicked it. The end of the semester was here, but studying for finals would have been a lot easier if I'd not been aware of the fact that Leo would be visiting his mom for the entire two weeks of Christmas break.

To add insult to injury, he was headed to Santa Barbara instead of Arizona. I couldn't believe it. Not only would we be apart—he'd be hanging out in my favorite beach town.

Memories of the house we used to rent on the sand

there every summer came floating back as if to taunt me... splashing in the waves, walking through the tide pools in the mornings with my mom. She knew the name of almost every seashell and taught me about the balance of sea life in each little pool.

I breathed deeply. The thought of Leo there without me was hard to take. *Click, click, click*, my pen sounded again.

"Shhh! Stop it. Focus." Jessie glared.

"Sorry," I said, laying my forehead on my notebook.

"Oh my gosh." Jessie rolled her eyes. "Let me guess. Leo's going to Arizona for Christmas. Woe is you."

The paper crumpled beneath my face as I shook my head. "That's the *thing*," my muffled voice moaned. "He's not going to Arizona. He's going to Santa Barbara. They're staying at a friend's cottage."

Jessie's face twisted. "*I'm* going to Santa Barbara, to see my grandparents."

"Don't rub it in," I said, lifting my head. "He'll be gone for Christmas *and* New Year's *and* my birthday," I groaned, now annoyed at the sound of my own whiny voice.

My birthday fell right in the middle of the holiday season, on December thirtieth, which was something I usually enjoyed. Not that I wanted a big eighteenth bash like Jessie, or anything. This year, the only thing I wanted was to spend at least part of the day with Leo.

"Okay, that *is* a bummer." Jessie gave a reluctant sideways nod, and then her face brightened. "Kai is having her Christmas party the day we get out of school... at least he'll be here for that!"

I stared at the floral bedspread, half listening. A second ticked by, and I sat up all of a sudden, my eyelids blinking rapidly.

"What?" Jessie asked.

A smile crept onto my face.

"Oh no." She frowned. "You have some sort of idea."

I moved my head up and down. "A brilliant one."

"No way."

"Why not?" I said, putting on my best offended-looking frown.

"Um, let's see, fifth grade comes to mind. The time when you insisted I hack all your hair off into a pixie cut like Audrey did in *Roman Holiday*?"

"You have to give me a break on that one—I was missing my mom!" I shrugged my head sideways and Jessie raised her eyebrows at me. "Okay it *was* a little drastic, but I loved that haircut."

"Yeah?" Jessie scoffed. "Well, your dad didn't, and my mom grounded me for a month." She rolled her eyes. "Hooray for Audrey."

I smothered a laugh and gave her a guilty grin. "But!" I pointed my finger in the air. "Audrey loved chocolate, which is what gave me the idea to smuggle Hershey's Kisses through your bedroom window every Saturday... did that make up for nothing?"

"Chocolate is never nothing. I forgot about that." She waved away my sheepish look. "Okay, you're forgiven."

"That was easy," I said swinging my feet over the side of the bed. "Okay, so—"

"No," she interrupted. "No ideas." She lifted a textbook, turning its pages. "You always end up getting off scot-free, and I'm the one who gets in trouble."

"That's not my fault! You're the Harvard-bound lawyer-to-be. You're going to have to work on your poker face." I edged off the bed toward her. "Seriously, just listen. You're going alone on the train when you go to your grandparents' house, right?"

Jessie looked from my right eye to my left eye and nodded slowly.

"Sooooo, I'll come with you to Santa Barbara, like I'm visiting them, too—and then I'll spend a day with Leo instead!" My heart began to beat faster.

"That. Is. So. Sneaky." Jessie's face was blank with seriousness. "No one would ever believe me if I told them how many devilish ideas were behind that angelic face." She shook her head, dismissing the idea. "Anyway, it won't work. I'm staying there for three days."

"Right! The day we get there, Leo picks me up at the train station—your grandparents won't even know I'm on the train. The next day, he drops me back at the train station and you pick me up as if I'm just arriving for a visit. They'll think I'm along for two days, and my dad will think I'm there for three!" I stopped, staring wide-eyed into the air at my brilliance.

Jessie's eyebrows arched to the ceiling. "You're going to spend the night with him?"

"C'mon, Jess." I rolled my eyes. "His mom is going to be there. It's a chance for... for like a mini-vacation in Santa Barbara!"

"A mini-vacation in Santa Barbara?" Jessie frowned. "Sounds suspiciously familiar to a mini-vacation in Rome."

I dipped my head to the side, admitting the truth of it. "But Audrey had such a great time in Rome! And I'm *positive* she didn't regret it." The desperate look on my face pleaded with her.

She looked away and back again. "I don't know. I guess it could work, Dovey."

"Yes, *yes!*" I jumped up, tackling her with a hug.

She laughed, pushing me away. "Okay, but if we get caught, you are going to take the heat for this—not me."

"We won't get caught!" I was sure of it. My stomach burned with excitement.

Jessie glanced at me sideways. "Wow. You are head over heels, girl."

Chapter 16

"I'VE HAD THE MOST TERRIBLE IMPULSE..."
-SABRINA FAIRCHILD

Sabrina

The train rattled along, shooting past grassy foothills on one side and long stretches of stormy beaches on the other. Wedged between a sleeping Jessie and the window, I peered into my book for the tenth time. I'd been on the same page for twenty minutes. I flipped it closed; it was no use. The combination of excitement and nervousness had my stomach in knots and my thoughts in turmoil. Not to mention the guilt I kept artfully ignoring. I was starting to wonder if it would all be worth it. After all, even though it was less than twenty-four hours together, how had I possibly thought it would be no big deal? And it didn't matter what my intentions were—if my dad found out I had spent the night with Leo, he would definitely assume the worst. All hell would break loose. I shifted in my seat. Had love made me stupid or something?

The rumbling continued as the train flew toward its destination. There was no turning back. Wishing now that I had brought a sketchpad, I leaned back and settled for staring out at the overcast sky above the ocean swells.

Visions of Kai's Christmas party swirled in my head. Leo and I had spent most of the time hanging out with everyone on the docks, watching the boat parade. Colorfully lit boats had cruised by while the music of holiday songs floated off the water, and muffled cries of, "Merry Christmas," blared from the captain's speakers of the large yachts. Leo must have kissed me thirty times.

I brought my hand to my cheek, feeling its warmth. Just remembering made me self-conscious. The truth was, I had surprised even myself. I thought back to when I'd been so annoyed by the two kids making out at the beach last summer. At Kai's party, the fact that half the senior class was milling around the yacht club hadn't been enough to stop my own make-out session. Every time Leo had turned to kiss me I'd melted, my head spinning in the sparkling darkness.

The train lurched into the station and pulled to a stop, waking Jessie with its jolt. She sat up and glanced around the train until her eyes met mine. Side by side, we gathered our bags in silence.

Jessie zipped her duffle, pulled it over her shoulder, and looked at me nervously. "Okay, I'll go out first. Make sure you wait long enough before you get off the train, so my grandma and grandpa don't see you."

"Thanks, Jess," I said, mustering my most confident look.

"Okay, text me." She squeezed my elbow. "We'll pick you up back here tomorrow morning at ten, so be waiting. I'll make us a little late to be on the safe side."

I gave her a thumbs-up, and she turned to make her way down the aisle.

Plunking myself back into the seat, I peered out the window, my eyes scanning the platform for Leo. My breath fogged the glass as a few raindrops fell, dotting the windowpane. I spotted Jessie's grandparents and slid down lower, peeking out from the bottom edge of the now-blurry window. They hugged Jessie and then turned to go, hurrying to escape the sudden showers.

I stood up and brushed myself off, part of me realizing that I was also trying to brush away the creepiness of sneaking around. My teeth gritted at the thought of it. Why did I have an incessant need for a crystal-clear conscience? It was time to break out of the trying-to-be-perfect mold once and for all.

With my bag over my shoulder, I made my way toward the door, peering out each windowpane I passed in hopes of catching sight of Leo. When I reached the doorway, I stopped for a moment to look out.

Right away, my eyes landed on a red Angels jersey. Leo stood on the platform directly in front of me, his arms crossed over his chest. The huge grin on his face said, *I can't believe you actually went through with this.*

I shot him a playful smirk as I stepped down, and he moved forward, weaving his way toward me. He reached out to grab my hand and pulled me to him. All around us, umbrellas opened as people hurried under the nearby arches of the train station, trying to escape the storm. The rain fell faster, but he ignored it, leaning in to kiss me.

With the rain now drenching us under the open sky, my insides jumped. It was as if we'd hopped straight into the famous *Breakfast at Tiffany's* scene I had watched so many times. Only this was better than I even imagined it would be. The touch of him against me, the electricity of his skin, the smell of his hair… I closed my eyes. It was all worth it.

Just the two of us remained on the empty platform now. Leo paused to look up at the pouring sky. Water trickled down his forehead when he lowered his chin, his fiery eyes roaming my face as though every single bit of it fascinated him.

I stood on my toes, blinking away the rain as I pulled him closer by his soaked jersey. "You really love this shirt, don't you?"

His eyes glinted, and he pulled me even closer, stopping his face only inches from mine. "Let's get this straight," he said. "I *like* the shirt." His breath was warm against my lips. "I *love* you."

LEO PULLED THE BRONCO to a stop in front of a small, white, craftsman cottage. The grass in the yard was wild and overgrown, but the porch was inviting with red geraniums spilling out of large, clay pots. The screen door swung open, and a pretty woman emerged, her straight brown hair brushing her shoulders. Opening an umbrella, she dashed down the steps and hurried to meet us halfway up the brick walk.

She greeted us with a friendly gasp and wrapped an arm around me as she pulled me underneath the umbrella. "Dove! I'm Susan. It's so nice to finally meet you. Leo hasn't stopped talking about you since he got here." She glanced at him, and he grinned as if to go along with her story as we climbed the steps to the front door.

Wood crackled in the brick fireplace beside two overstuffed loveseats in the small living room. I turned toward the fire, welcoming the heat as it warmed my skin through my soaked clothes. Susan took hold of my bag and rounded the corner into a small hallway to the right.

"Dove, you'll be in here," her voice echoed from the bedroom. She emerged back through the doorway, her arms empty. "And you'll be there, Leo." She pointed to one of the couches and locked eyes with him.

Leo gave her a casual shrug, and I excused myself into the bedroom, eager to escape the awkward moment. I had to hand it to Susan, she sure didn't waste any time getting to the point.

My eyes darted over to the bed as I peeled off my wet clothes and put on a dry pair of jeans and my blue sweater. Part of me couldn't help feeling disappointed. I *had* hoped that we would be able to sleep next to each other. The idea of at least holding him and feeling him breathe all night was a temptation I had planned on giving in to.

I pulled on my navy coat and headed back to the living room, declaring myself ready to face the storm.

"Oh!" Susan smiled at us. "I made reservations for you two at a restaurant in the harbor," she said in an extra friendly way, as though trying to soften the earlier blow. "I thought you might like to eat on the water."

"Sounds great—thank you." My eyes shot to Leo, who was now sporting a jacket and dry pants.

"Perfect." He jumped up from his seat by the fire, grabbed the car keys in one hand, and stretched his other hand out toward me. "Let's go see Santa Barbara."

RAINFALL HINDERED THE VIEWS of the city on our ride through town, but it didn't matter. In fact, it gave a magical, misty ambiance to the already special feeling of being alone together away from home. It was like an aura surrounding us—bonding us even closer. Still, in the back of my mind, worry grated. What if we saw someone we knew? It wasn't like Santa Barbara was Siberia. There *was* a possibility of running into someone who might blow the whole thing.

"There's East Beach," Leo said, pointing out at the waves.

The Bronco sped through the rain as I pointed out the zoo on the opposite side. "I loved going there when I was little."

He looked straight ahead as he drove along. "You were a cute kid."

"Like you ever noticed." I rolled my eyes.

"I noticed!" His forehead wrinkled.

"No you did not!" I tilted my head back, laughing. "You never said a word to me—"

"I was shy around you!"

"Oh right! You? Shy around girls? Please."

He let out a breath, shaking his head as he stared at the road through the back and forth of the windshield wipers.

"Am I right?" I asked, fishing for more.

"You did your state report on Pennsylvania," he said quietly. "When you stood in front of the class, you kept brushing a piece of hair out of your face, and I remember thinking how perfect you were—pretty and smart."

I had to make an effort not to let my mouth drop open.

"You always seemed... sad though," he said, looking over. "About your mom."

I took a slow breath and nodded at the memories of my mom in her hospital bed. Fifth grade had not been

125

an easy year.

"And... you seemed unattainable." He shrugged. "Like an angel or something."

I shook my head at him, my eyes wide. The whole time. The whole time I had a crush on him he had felt the same way. I let his sentence replay in my head and had the sudden urge to laugh at the ridiculousness of being compared to an angel, but his serious look reined me in. I reached out to grab his hand. "Well, I'm glad you came to your senses—and now you know first-hand that I am definitely not an angel."

He chuckled and then pointed out at the wharf as we pulled to a stop behind a row of cars at a red light. Outside my window, a restaurant was packed with people. Apparently, the fact that it was pouring rain hadn't stopped the tourists or the locals from heading out to dinner.

My eyes focused in on the crowded tables. A flash of a girl's dark hair and sharp profile caught my eye, and I whipped my head further to the right. Was that Piper? I strained to get a better look, squinting as the Bronco lurched and started forward again. The restaurant faded from sight, and I sat up straight, my eyes darting around me at nothing in particular as I tried to absorb the possibility. There was no way. No way Piper was here. It was paranoia, pure and simple.

Leo steered the truck into the marina entrance. I tried my best to ignore the fluttering in my stomach as we pulled into the parking lot and then dashed up the stairway to the restaurant, ducking to avoid the downpour.

Seated at a small table in the corner, we ordered clam chowder and fish 'n' chips while the storm continued outside. Every few minutes, I glanced around the crowded room, scanning for anyone I might know. If I *might* have seen Piper, then I *might* see anyone else, right? It just made the likelihood seem like more of a possibility now.

After ignoring my anxious looks the first few minutes, Leo finally let out an exasperated breath. "Dove. Relax. No one is going to recognize you."

"Yeah, I know," I said. "I just, you know... want to make sure."

He leaned back in his chair. "So, what's going on with your art lately?" His attempt to get my mind off it was obvious, but charming.

"Not a lot. There's an art show at school in the spring, so I'm going to help with that."

His face softened, and he raised his eyebrows as though he wanted to hear more.

I let out a self-conscious laugh. "Um, let's see... I've kind of been into watercolors lately."

"Why have I never seen you paint or draw anything?" He frowned.

"What? I've shown you my paintings—"

"Yeah, but I've never actually seen you in action." He flipped over one of the paper placemats in front of us. A few greasy stains had soaked through, but otherwise it was a blank, white page.

"C'mon. Go. Draw that." He pointed out the window to the bay. Rain still poured down, pelting the moored boats clustered in the harbor. In the distance, the ocean sprawled out into the darkness.

I threw up my hands. "With what?"

Leo looked around. A family was sitting together at the table next to us, the youngest boy coloring away at his kid's menu. Leo leaned toward him. "Hey, can we borrow one of those?" he asked, pointing to a small cup filled with crayons. The boy studied him for a moment, then reached into the cup and handed him a blue crayon.

"Thanks." He leaned back to our table and presented me with the prize. "Here you go. Let's see what you got."

I took the crayon and began to sketch, my eyes darting out the window and back to the paper over and again. Leo watched the boats in the harbor take shape on the page, then the rock jetty behind them, along with the nuances of the stormy sea and the mountains in the distance.

I finished, turning it around to face him.

"Wow."

"Thanks," I said as he studied my drawing. "I used to sketch the tide pools here every summer. We stayed at a cottage on the coolest little beach—Miramar Beach. My mom and I would climb around the rocks when the tide was low. There's a ton of sea life in them."

The door to the restaurant flew open, and the sound of the rain outside grew louder. I spun around. Two people came in, shaking the water from their coats and umbrellas. My stare lingered longer than necessary until I finally decided their faces weren't familiar.

All of a sudden, my phone buzzed, making me jump before I fumbled to read the text.

Don't dive under the table.

I looked up at Leo. He was holding his phone in his hand, laughing.

Chapter 17

"So, I've spent the night here with you?"
-Princess Ann

Roman Holiday

My eyes fluttered open. Leo was standing beside the bed. It was still dark in the room, but outside the window, a bit of orange light peeked through the sky.

"Hey, Birdy." He had that sweet look on his face again—the one that made me feel like I was some sort of goddess, unaware of my hidden identity. "C'mon." His head motioned toward the door. "I want to show you something." He tossed his flannel hoodie at me, and I caught it, throwing it on over my T-shirt and gray sweats. We tiptoed to the front door and slipped out into the morning.

"Where are we going?" I asked, grabbing his hand. His fingers were warm and strong as they closed around mine.

"You'll see," he answered, his tone rising and falling mysteriously.

We turned and headed down a small, sandy path

bordered by overgrown plants and shrubs. The sound of rushing water came toward us as the empty beach opened up ahead. A flock of gulls was sleeping on the sand in the distance, and farther out, a sandpiper darted around at the shoreline.

I burst into a run. "Oh my gosh! This is Miramar Beach!" I stopped, surveying the long curve of homes sitting side by side along the beachfront. "This is where we used to stay when I was a kid—I had no idea we were so close! This is the *same* beach!" I repeated in disbelief. "That's the cottage right there!" I pointed to a little green house with a brown-shingled roof. Beach towels were thrown over the chairs outside, and a Boogie Board leaned against the porch railing.

Leo beamed at me and rubbed the back of his head. I paused, watching and waiting for his hand to linger on his neck. When it did, he pointed with his other hand off to the right, where the rocks jutted out of the cliffs and onto the beach. "So then I guess you already know that the tide pools are around that curve."

"Let's go!" I exclaimed as I turned and ran out toward the rocky shoreline. Sunrise was in full force now, with half a brilliant orange ball emerging from the skyline. The gulls woke, startled, and flew away into the sun.

Leo's feet pounded the sand behind me. He caught up and bumped me hard with his shoulder as we ran, knocking me off-balance and taking the lead.

"Not fair!" I shouted.

He slowed to a jog, laughing as I rounded the bend behind him. Large formations of rocks spanned ahead of us at the shoreline. Beyond them, waves crashed, sending white foamy water to wash through the pools.

I hopped onto the wet rocks, choosing my footing carefully between the jagged edges and slippery, flat surfaces. The little crevices were brimming with sea life, and I looked into each one as I passed and then stopped, bending down to check out one of the smaller pools. "Come see these!"

Leo made his way over to me, and I pointed at a group of purple urchins clustered together. He didn't say a word, but his crooked smile was self-satisfied. I finally got it. This was why we had woken so early.

"You knew it was low tide, didn't you?" I asked.

His dimples appeared as he teased me with his eyes. I grabbed his hand and pulled him behind me as we slipped and hopped our way back over the rocks. When we reached the sand, I turned and leaned into him, pushing him onto his back. His eyes closed as I pressed my mouth against his, and he wrapped his arms firmly around me, his fingers finding their way under my shirt to the skin of my back, pulling me tightly to him.

My breath caught against his mouth as I weaved my hand through the hair on the back of his head, massaging it the way he always did, the way I always watched him do. Only this time I owned the movement. Waves crashed in my ears as I let my fingers follow the same path his always did, curving down to the back of his neck.

A dog's bark broke the solitary sound of the waves on the sand, and we turned our heads to see two people with a Labrador walking toward us at the water's edge. I sat up and smoothed my hair as they came closer. They nodded as they passed, their feet making imprints in the wet sand, erasing our atmosphere of aloneness. In the distance, several more people began to dot the shoreline.

Leo sat up beside me, brushing the sand from his shirt in silence. I leaned against his shoulder, not wanting the closeness of the moment to end. "Last night, I wished I could sleep next to you."

He bent his head to mine. "I wanted to do more than that," he whispered against my ear.

My stomach fluttered at the prospect of more than that, and the beat of my heart picked up again.

The heat from his breath moved to my neck as he kissed it slowly. "*Someday…*" his lips moved lower to the skin of my throat, and I shivered as he continued, "*someday…* we'll have a bedroom together." His mouth found mine again, and his kiss, though still slow, was fiery now. As though its purpose was to translate everything he felt. He slowed to a stop, and I opened my eyes to his face hovering, unmoving, in front of mine. "When that happens…" he said, pulling me closer, "we won't leave it for days and days."

I laid my head against him and buried my cheek into the warmth of his jacket. The future. I turned to stare out at the rushing water. The long-term future. He was actually planning it. With me. *Someday.* The word floated through my head again. *Someday.*

The sun was higher in the sky now, with only a few smaller clouds lingering from the night before—an annoying reminder that I'd have to leave soon. More and more, every moment we spent together felt stolen, as if our lives were not our own and the real world was chasing us. In front of me, the waves rose and crashed over and again, voicing all the turmoil I felt inside.

Why did life seem to always be pulling us apart? The idea gnawed at the silence, and I tossed my hair in the breeze, trying to toss the nagging thought away, too.

Off to the left, another person was walking toward us at the water's edge, and I glanced over, ready to nod hello. My stomach flipped at the sight of the dark-haired girl who had now stopped in her tracks a few feet away.

"Piper!" The name jumped out of my mouth as I scrambled to stand. Leo stood, too, shooting me a look.

Wide-eyed, Piper didn't move. "Hi." She sounded almost as shocked as I felt.

"What are you doing here?" I shifted my feet and wished the question hadn't popped out so guilty-sounding. My eyes moved to the sketchpad she held at her hip. "Oh! Are you going to sketch the tide pools?" I cringed at the overly energetic sound of my voice. *Stop babbling.*

Piper pointed down the beach to a large, white cottage at the end of the row of homes. "My parents rented a beach house here."

Her tone wasn't half as horrible as I thought it would be, especially since she still hadn't spoken to me since that day she accused me of stealing Leo. I tried to steady my breath, attempting to make myself sound as casual as possible. "Oh, that's nice. My family used to come here, too."

My heart wouldn't stop beating wildly. This was a nightmare. The only worse person to run into on this beach would have been Clarissa. I fought away a blurry-eyed, dizzy feeling as the consequences of being caught began to materialize in my head. If Piper told anyone or posted anything about this, it would become *the* Bayport High gossip, and chances were good that my dad would find out. That was if Piper didn't just go directly to him and tell him herself.

She flicked her gaze up and down at me. "What are *you* doing here?" Her eyes moved to Leo and back to me again.

The question seemed to hang in the air even though I answered as quickly as possible. "I'm just spending a few days up here with Jessie and her grandparents."

The awkward quiet seemed to strangle me, tensing my entire body. *Composure. Poise.* My hands began to shake, and I crossed my arms in front of me, suddenly remembering with a pang of panic that I was wearing Leo's flannel hoodie. This was so bad.

"Really?" Her eyes flitted to Leo again. "That's... not what it looks like."

And there it was. The snide, I've-caught-you-now comment. Still, she wasn't half as awful as she could have been. But, that was Piper. She'd always been the type of friend who was an enigma. Sometimes she came across as cool and friendly, making you believe she might have potential as a decent person, and other times she was just plain mean. And then there was my personal favorite: when she was sweet yet rude, all at the same time.

I clenched my jaw and tried to smile. "Leo and I are just spending the morning together." I glanced over, and he gave a casual shrug. "And, um, I'm headed back to Jessie's now, actually." I turned to Leo again, the tension now excruciating. "Yeah... so, we'd better go, right?"

Before he could answer, Piper brushed past us, flipping open her sketchpad. "Yeah, I think you'd better."

Chapter 18

"PLEASE, DARLING, DON'T SIT THERE LOOKING AT
ME LIKE THAT."
-HOLLY GOLIGHTLY

Breakfast at Tiffany's

The morning sun filtered through the white crepe curtains in my cushioned window seat. It was December thirtieth. My eighteenth birthday. I was supposed to be considered an adult now, but the idea seemed almost ridiculous. Adults were mature and made rational decisions—unlike me and my insane Santa Barbara scheme. I'd made the trip back to Newport the night before with Jessie, during which I'd done nothing but drive her crazy by stressing over Piper. For the last two days Piper had dominated my thoughts, twisting my stomach into knots.

There were too many variables to do any proper sort of damage control. I had considered a hundred different scenarios, including calling Piper and asking her not to say anything, but the idea of actually going through with it was unbearable. Besides, her snarky goodbye had really irked me. *Yeah, I think you'd better.*

How dare she say it as though I were doing something wrong. I peeked through the curtains at a small electric Duffy boat chugging along through the bay. Okay, so I *had* been doing something wrong. Technically. But there were reasons. And it was none of Piper's business. It certainly wasn't anything to warrant her talking down to me as if she were morally superior or something.

"Do-ove." My stepmom's voice sang out my name in two syllables, and I braced myself for her saccharine happiness. She rapped once on the bedroom door before it swung open and her head poked into the room. But instead of her usual wide-eyed grin, her smile seemed hesitant.

"Happy birthday!" She walked straight to the window seat to draw back the curtains. Sunlight beamed in, brightening the entire room.

I closed my eyes against the glaring light as Patty perched beside me. She clasped her hands in her lap, looking down at them before she spoke. "You've seemed distant lately." I shifted, readying my defenses as she continued, "And I'm sorry for that. I feel like it's our fault, with—with your dad's decision about Leo and all..."

Tears quickly welled. *Yes, it is your fault.* I wanted to blurt it out, make her pay for all the crazy chaos and worry that now whipped through my life like a daily tornado. I frowned but managed a small nod.

"Thank you." She dipped her head, the worried look on her face not vanishing. "For understanding." It was a terrible choice of words. After all, I *didn't* understand. I never would. "So, your dad wanted..." she hesitated. "Well, *we* wanted to give you something special for your birthday this year—"

"That's really not necessary, Patty," I interrupted.

136

How about giving me the gift of independence and trust? I would much prefer that.

I hopped up and into my bathroom to grab my toothbrush, wanting to change the subject but unable to come up with anything. My thoughts ping-ponged. Here Patty was, making an effort to connect with me and apologize for my dad, and I had just snuck around behind their backs like a lovesick, crazy person.

"Well, we're all waiting in the kitchen for you." She flashed another nervous smile and shrugged as she stood. "So come on down when you're ready."

"Okay," I answered, scrubbing my front teeth. Time to go downstairs and accept a gift for being the perfect daughter that I wasn't. "I'll be right there."

MY DAD LOOKED UP from where he stood hovered over the stove, smiling. "Morning, baby." If I could have sighed out loud I would have. He was making his famous specialty breakfast just for me.

"Morning." I leaned into the burners, eyeing the omelets. "They better not be heart-healthy today," I said, faking an evil stare.

He pointed to the bowl of beaten eggs. "Absolutely not. I used every yolk—but they can wait a minute," he said, turning the heat down on the burner. "We want to show you something."

He wiped his hands on a red-striped dishtowel and threw it over his shoulder in chef-like fashion.

I followed him through the kitchen to the backdoor, stopping at the sight of Jessie waiting next to Griffin. They were both leaning back against the door—guarding it almost.

"Jess!" My eyes darted from one face to the other. "What's… going on?"

"Hey—Happy birthday!" Jessie raised her eyebrows, giving me a mischievous smirk.

"Close your eyes!" Griffin grinned.

I squinted at all of them, frowned, and then shielded my eyes with my hand. I heard the backdoor open and the electric sound of the garage door lifting.

Griffin tugged on my free hand, leading me out through the garage. "Keep them closed!"

We stepped outside onto the front driveway, and Jessie and Griffin pulled me to a stop as my thoughts continued to race. What kind of present could this possibly be? "Seriously, what's going on?"

"Okay!" Griffin announced. "You can look now!"

I let my hand drop and opened my eyes. A small, silver Fiat was parked in the driveway, its convertible top pulled back to reveal gray leather seats glowing in the sunshine.

My stomach flipped, but I just stood there, frozen.

Patty let out a laugh. "Happy birthday!"

"And happy early graduation," my dad chimed in. "It's not new, but it's in nice condition and the engine's a good one." He dipped his head, shrugging. "Should get great mileage."

In a million years, I never would have guessed this. A car. A car. A *convertible*. For as long as I could remember, my dad had been completely clear about teenagers and car ownership—that I'd have to enjoy Jessie's good fortune, because it wasn't going to happen for me. This gift was a complete one-eighty. My gut tightened. It was also completely too much. Not to mention too… wrong? I had spent the last four months following my heart instead of my dad's orders. Now, here he was, patting me on the head for complying with his wishes. My stomach churned.

I turned to Jessie, my eyes wide. She grabbed both of my hands, jumping up and down. Griffin ran toward the car, squealing as he circled it. I squeezed Jessie's fingers, slowing her down. "Jess." I looked sideways toward my dad. He was standing with Patty, laughing with her at Griffin's yelps of joy. I shook my head back and forth at Jessie with as little movement as possible. "It feels… weird," I whispered, frowning.

Jessie's brow furrowed. She leaned in closer. "Are you insane?" She looked over at my parents and faked a huge smile, then let out a loud whoop. "It's amazing!" She waved at them and then turned back to me, her fake smile not wavering. "Isn't it amazing?" she said through gritted teeth. She leaned in closer, now scowling. "Think Audrey in *Sabrina*. Top down. William Holden. Wind in her hair." She nodded, coaxing me along. "Get in the car, Dove."

My gaze moved to my dad and Patty as I stepped toward the car, making an effort to smile in their direction before opening the door to slide onto the warm seat. Griffin ran around the front bumper and climbed into the back as Jessie hopped into the passenger seat, slamming the door.

I gripped the wheel, and the picture of Audrey's smiling face surfaced in my mind, her scarf blowing behind her in the breeze while the little convertible zipped along. I turned to Jessie as a genuine smile emerged.

Jessie's eyes widened as she gave me a knowing smirk. She flicked her head toward my parents. "Say something," she whispered.

I turned toward Patty and my dad. They stood

together, beaming, looking so proud of themselves... so proud of *me*. "Thank you!" I called out. "Thank you... so much..." I felt my smile start to fade, but I bit my lip and forced it back into place.

Chapter 19

"SECRET?"
-SABRINA FAIRCHILD

Sabrina

On the first day of the new semester, the art room buzzed with its usual chaotic energy. Each rectangular art table had been arranged with a pair of chairs and a bowl of fruit. As Jessie and I made our way to two open seats, an airy giggle floated toward us. Before looking up, I knew exactly whose laugh it was. I let my eyes drift sideways. Clarissa stood across the room with her phone angled in front of some fruit, taking one picture after another. Her next post, no doubt. How many likes would her random bowl of fruit get? At least three hundred, and probably all from guys who wished they could lay their eyes on a lot more than her fruit picture.

Ms. Atkins rapped a pencil on her table at the front of the class, and everyone took their seats as a hush settled over the classroom. "Okay, ladies and gentlemen, thank you for joining me in a brand-new art class offered here at Bayport High this semester: Charcoal and Chalk

Pastels, where we'll have the chance to explore these two mediums. Some of you are old hat at all of this, others are new to the world of art. If that's you, then welcome."

I leaned into Jessie. "Yes, welcome."

Jessie didn't crack a smile. "I cannot believe you talked me into this."

"More than anything," Ms. Atkins looked upward, carefully choosing her words, "I'm hoping to help you learn more about art and more about yourself on this journey we are about to take together."

Jessie glared sideways at me and pretended to gag. "What is she talking about?" she whispered. "This is not a journey, it's a stupid art class."

I choked back a laugh as Ms. Atkins's voice droned on in a serious tone. "I'm not here to teach you how to draw. I'm here to teach you how to see—to see everything from a new perspective. It is my hope that by the time April rolls around, each and every one of you will have a piece of artwork you will be proud to display at our spring art show."

Jessie dropped her forehead onto the desk. She rolled her head sideways toward me. "*Why* did I sign up for this?"

I looked down at my paper, starting the first strokes with a charcoal pencil. "Because you agreed that an art class on your final transcript would show off how truly well-rounded you are."

She blinked. "True... and a hundred percent unnecessary. I completely regret it now."

The two girls sitting in front of us turned their heads and looked at me, then at each other, their voices lowered to a whisper. I tightened my grip on my pencil. What was that all about? Did they know something? All day long I'd analyzed and reanalyzed people's attitudes and reactions, trying to find out whether Piper had spilled the story or not. All it would have taken was one text to unleash a rumor.

"Hi, Jude," I tossed out to the girl on the left, hoping to start a conversation to ease my crazy fears.

Jude turned her head. "Hi, Dove." She barely managed a smile and then spun back around to face her own drawing table. So much for a conversation. I bit the inside of my cheek, forcing my eyes back to the paper in front of me. I'd known Jude since the third grade, and no matter how many friendly attempts I'd thrown out, she always seemed to have something against me.

Jessie moved her charcoal against her paper, staring at the bowl in front of her as if it were filled with crawling worms instead of fresh fruit. From the front of the room came a soft giggle. Clarissa again.

"I can't believe she's in this class," Jessie said, eyeing Clarissa over the fruit. "How jealous would she be if she knew about you and Leo in Santa Barbara?"

I glanced up toward Jude. "Shhh!" I snapped at Jessie as my eyes circled the room in one sweep. "Take it down a notch, Jess. I'm freaked out."

Jessie lowered to a whisper as she tried to sketch an apple. "I still can't believe that whole plan went smoothly. I mean, really, you've had a few crazy ideas through the years, but let's face it, you've essentially been a goody-goody your entire life. I don't know whether I should be happy for you or really start to worry."

I narrowed my eyes at her, half-joking, and Jessie fell silent, using all of her concentration to draw the outline of some grapes hanging over the edge of the bowl.

Jude and her friend didn't look back again for the rest of the class, and my fears eased a little as I finished my drawing and started to clean up. The classroom filled with the growing buzz of talking as everyone began to pack up their things.

"Ugh," Jude blurted from the table in front of us. "I have to go to work now." She stood, lifting her bag onto her shoulder. "I have to actually work to pay for things—unlike some people, whose lives consist of making out on docks and racing around in convertibles."

I tried to wrap my head around her not-so-subtle dig before I scoffed audibly. Wow, she was annoying, with her pinched face and judgmental sneer. I just couldn't let it go. "Uh, I'm sitting right here, Jude."

Jude snapped her head around, flitting her eyes up and down the length of me. "I wasn't talking about you, Dove. You don't have to be so defensive."

I turned away, rolling my eyes. I would take ten Pipers over one Jude. At least Piper had the guts to say whatever it was to your face. The only way to fight back against Jude's snide remarks was to throw a personal attack right back—but in a sneaky way, of course. That was the passive-aggressive game... you had to be able to deny everything.

The bell rang. *Whatever.* Today I didn't feel like fighting her stupid battle. I closed my eyes, doing my best to shove away the grinding annoyance and somehow tap into my inner Audrey. Time to take the high road. *Composure. Poise.* With my head held high, I stood and grabbed my bag alongside Jessie. "See ya," I called out to Jude with as much niceness as I could muster.

We headed out the classroom door, making our way across the campus to the parking lot. In the distance, Greta and Nate were walking hand in hand toward us. Greta waved and picked up her pace. Her long, flowery skirt billowed behind her as she turned over her shoulder to Nate. "You go ahead! I just want to talk to Dove real quick. I'll catch up."

She stopped in front of us, flipping her purple bangs with a flick of her head, but they fell right back into a perfect, thick line across her forehead. "You guys should know something."

I braced myself. "Okay." My stomach tightened. "What is it?"

"There's some serious gossip going around." Her eyes darted sideways. "Last night, Jude posted this rumor that you snuck away to Santa Barbara to be with Leo over the break. Everyone's joking around that you had this big lover's tryst."

Fantastic. Every bell that had gone off in my brain telling me to be worried had been right. Jessie blinked at me and then fumbled for her phone.

"Don't bother looking for it." Greta shook her head. "She already deleted it. I have no idea why."

I stared blankly at Greta for a moment as the shock sank in, and then shot her a smile. "Thanks Greta. I'd better not confirm or deny it, if you know what I mean."

Greta laughed in her laid-back way and waved goodbye over her head as she ran off to catch up with Nate. Jessie and I exchanged glances and quickly headed to my car.

"I knew it," I said, opening the driver's door. "I *knew* Piper would do this. She just couldn't wait to get revenge."

"Maybe not," Jessie said as she slipped into the passenger seat. "It could have come from someone else—accidentally. Like, Clive and Isaiah knew, right? Maybe one of them told someone in secret. You know how everyone always has that one person they swear to secrecy? Well, after a chain of ten secret keepers, it could just fly out of control."

I shook my head as I started the car, putting it into gear. "I doubt it." The fact was that it didn't matter. There really was no one to blame but myself. I'd gotten myself into this crazy mess, now I'd just have to be hyper-vigilant and deal with it. I steered the Fiat out of the parking lot, staring ahead without a word.

"I take that back... it wouldn't have been Isaiah," Jessie said quietly. "I'm pretty much the only one he ever told secrets to."

"Do you... miss him?" I asked, treading carefully. Jessie had never been the touchy-feely type, especially about her own feelings—and especially about guys. But Isaiah was special to her. He always had been.

"Yeah, sometimes," she answered.

"Tell him." I threw it out, hoping it might stick.

"No. *He* broke up with *me*, remember? Besides, we're good as friends."

I studied the road ahead of me, forcing myself not to say anything else. They were good as friends, yes—but *great* as a couple.

Jessie flipped the sun visor down in front of her face and looked into the mirror. "Wanna come over?"

"No thanks, I'm going to watch Leo at batting practice later."

"Mmmm, sounds riveting." She chuckled, flipping the visor closed. When I didn't laugh, she snapped into serious mode again. "Try not to worry, Dove."

"It's not just that... it's... Jude." I rubbed my forehead. "I can't stand her."

"Jude?" Jessie faked a serious look. "Oh, you mean Rude Jude, the Annoying Prude?"

I let out a reluctant laugh. "That is so immature,

Jess." As much as I hated to admit it, Jude's remarks had cut deep. "Why would she post something about me? And did you hear what she said about my car?"

"Seriously? Don't even sweat it. C'mon, it's Psych 101. She's *jealous*. She wants to paint you as lame and superficial so she can feel better about herself."

I bit my lip sideways, thinking. It would be so easy to go with that angle—there *was* probably some truth to it. Still, maybe what Jude said was true, too. "This is why I wanted to use the Paris money I saved to buy my own car." I glanced over at Jessie. "I hate people judging me."

Jessie snorted, and in that moment, I wished I had one ounce of her moxie.

"You have a convertible. Big deal," she declared in her snappy, debate-team voice. She breathed in sharply and paused, pointing her finger in the air. "You know who would want you to enjoy it?" She smiled knowingly. "Your mom. Your mom would have loved this car. I'm telling you... ignore the likes of Jude."

I leaned back against the headrest. I wasn't exactly sure about all of it, but I hoped Jessie was right. She sure was convincing. "You're going to make a great lawyer someday."

She laughed, flicking her eyebrows upward. "I know."

EVENING FOG DRIFTED IN toward the baseball field from over the cliffs, its cloud-like billows lingering in the air and then disappearing as they wafted past. The soft grass of the field flattened beneath my feet as I made my way across to the batting cages. I could distinctly hear the thump of the baseball bat and the clinking sound the ball made when it slammed against the chain-link fencing. All the cages stood empty except one. Inside it, Leo swung the bat over and over as he talked to a teammate feeding baseballs one-by-one into the machine.

I sat down to watch on a nearby bench, and after twenty minutes I still hadn't tired at the sight of his body twisting as he swung with all his force. After a while, he glanced at his watch and then over at me. He shouted to his buddy, and they quickly packed up, closing the cage behind them.

With one hand, he took off his helmet as he walked across the damp grass toward me.

He was giving me that look again—the something's-special-about-Dove look. Sweat dripped from his hair, and his right eyebrow fell lower than the left as he smiled at me.

"Hey!" He continued his stride toward me, his tight-fitting baseball clothes outlining every inch of his body. "Great news. The scout from the Giants contacted my coach again. They're still really interested, and he's coming to see me play again." He stood in front of me, grinning and out of breath.

My stomach jumped. This was really happening. He would be drafted into a major league team in June, and then what? Where would I go to school? Would I even get in anywhere? How would it all work out? I breathed in and faked a smile. "That's great."

"Yeah." He grabbed the back of his neck, not bothering to rub the back of his head this time. "I don't know if my dad will be happy, though. He keeps hoping for the Angels or the Cardinals to take an interest in me. I mean, I'd love that, too, but the Giants are a great team."

We turned, walking toward the parking lot together. "When you get accepted to that school you like in San Francisco, it'll be perfect, right?"

"Yeah." I answered, trying my best to sound cheerful.

"What?" he panted. "What is it?"

"I just… I don't know which schools are going to accept me, and you don't know for sure where you'll be drafted. It's all so up in the air."

He put his arm around me, slowing his pace. "Stop worrying so much. We love each other. That's what matters. It's all going to work out."

"But what if it doesn't? And rumors are flying around about me going to Santa Barbara with you. If my dad finds out, Leo—"

"He's not going to find out, Dove. Does he go to Bayport High? It's just a few people talking." He stopped in front of my car, leaning against it. "Thank God you finally got some wheels, Birdy."

I shrugged, smiling. "Yeah." Having my own car made it a lot easier to see Leo now—an ironic fact that never stopped grating my conscience.

"Makes me wonder sometimes, though… how many guys shout at you now that you're driving around in your convertible?"

"You don't need to worry about that," I answered, frowning. "Now who's the one worrying?"

He moved closer, still breathing heavily, his hair falling onto his forehead and sweeping over his eyes. I could smell the salt on his skin as he moved his face to within centimeters of mine. My eyes closed halfway, waiting for his lips, but he just stood there, unmoving. His breath warmed my mouth as some sort of invisible electricity pulled between us.

Scanning his face, I smiled to myself as I realized

what was going on. He was playing a game. His eyes stared at my lips, but he succeeded in holding back. My heart began to race, and my breath caught as I managed to resist the overwhelming urge to close the one-inch gap to feel the warmth of his mouth and the strength of his body against mine. He made a small sound— the tiniest, wanting sigh, and what little resolve I had quickly crumbled. I reached out and gripped him to me, pressing my mouth to his. He grabbed me tightly, his quick response rewarding me as his entire body wrapped around mine.

Chapter 20

Roman Holiday

The baseball diamond at Bayport High was situated close to the school, near the Dover Cliffs above the dirt trails and marshes of the Back Bay inlet waters. On the first Friday afternoon in March, a breeze blew over the bluffs as the stands began to fill for the opening game of the season. Out on the field, the players in uniform warmed up, throwing balls and taking practice swings. They all looked the same from a distance, wearing white baseball pants and navy-blue jerseys with *Pirates* emblazoned in white letters across the front.

The bleachers were packed with spectators, and I walked slowly up the cement steps, searching for a familiar face before spotting Isaiah sitting with Clive a few rows over. I waved to catch Isaiah's attention, and he waved back at me as I edged my way toward them.

"Is that Dove?" A deep voice to my right rang out.

I turned to take in the sight of a tall man with bits of gray speckled through his slick, dark hair. "Mr.

Donovan!"

"No, no, call me Mike." He turned to a man sitting beside him. "This is Leo's girlfriend. She's a beauty, isn't she?"

I swallowed hard, resisting the urge to scowl at him. *I'm not a horse. I'm a person—and I'm standing right here.* His rude comment was not only sexist, but over the top—there were plenty of girls at Bayport who were prettier. I collected myself. This was Leo's dad. I'd just have to suck it up. He only meant it as a compliment, I assured myself, and at least he was trying to be friendly.

I gave him the Audrey-lifted chin and found a polite smile.

"So, our boy is batting cleanup today, huh? He's going to impress those scouts this year, I'm telling you." His eyes looked through me, not at me, as though he were talking more to his friend or to himself rather than to me.

I bobbed my head like I knew exactly what batting cleanup meant and made casual conversation until I could wedge in a courteous excuse and a goodbye. Moving on through the bleachers, I finally made it to the seat beside Isaiah.

"Hi, guys." I let out a breath before I sat down.

"Hey," Isaiah said, moving over to make room. "Where's Jessie?"

Interesting. Something about it seemed like more than just a friendly question. "She had some stuff going on with the debate team," I answered, making a mental note to mention it to Jessie later.

I scanned the field. Leo was standing on the diamond next to third base with a glove dangling from his hand and a navy cap shielding his face. All the warm-ups had stopped now, and the players had moved to their positions. It looked like the game was about to start.

"Can you tell me what batting cleanup means?" I asked, turning to Isaiah.

"Oh, yeah." He gave me a sideways smile as though it was cute that I had no clue whatsoever about baseball lingo. "That's what you call it when someone bats fourth in the lineup, like Leo does," he added with a wink. He pointed out at home plate. "The idea is that the batters in front of him will get on base." He moved his arm, pointing at first base, then second base. "Then he'll clean up the bases by batting them in. It's usually the most powerful hitter."

Clive leaned into Isaiah, pointing and commenting as the stands became more crowded around us. Off to the right, I spotted Piper sitting with a few girls. She looked deep in conversation, her dark hair glistening in the sun. Anger welled up at the idea of being so betrayed by her. Yes, we'd had a weird competition thing since the sixth grade, when it had been a matter of who could draw a better unicorn. But despite that— or perhaps even because of it—I had always felt that I had a cohort in the world of art. A rival cohort, but a cohort all the same. Piper challenged me, but never in a horrible way. In fact, there had been enough friendly times through the years to make me believe that she would never hurt me on purpose. Try her hardest to win in a competition? Yes. But try to destroy my life with a nasty rumor? I never would have thought so.

Movement on the field caught my attention while cheering and shouting started up in the stands as the game began. Leo's body moved with natural skill as he dived and jumped for the ball, easily throwing the runners out at first base.

At the bottom of the first inning, he walked to the plate as the fourth batter. For a brief moment, he held the bat in one hand and grabbed the back of his neck with the other. My stomach fluttered nervously for him. He tapped the bat on the ground, held it over his right shoulder and waited. Swinging it forward, he smacked the first pitch, hitting it foul into the stands. A bunch of people stood to catch it as he resumed his stance.

The second pitch seemed to soar at him in slow motion. I clenched my fists, willing him to hit the ball. A split second later, either the magic had worked or he hadn't needed my help at all, because he hit the ball square in the middle of his bat, sending it soaring into the center of the field. Everyone in the stands erupted into a roar as the ball dropped and rolled across the grass toward the fence. His teammate on base came in to score, while Leo rounded the plate at first and ran toward second.

Isaiah leaned over to me, raising his voice to be heard over the shouting. "And that's how you bat cleanup!"

I clapped along with the crowd, my eyes staying fixed on him as he slid into second base.

Up and off to the left, a group of guys kept on shouting, longer and louder than the rest of the crowd. I turned to get a better look, and my insides jumped. There, laughing alongside the group was Clarissa. Great. First Piper, now Clarissa. *The gang's all here.*

"I know him!" One of the big football guys in a letterman's jacket pumped his fist in the air. "I know him! That's my buddy Leo!"

I didn't recognize him at all. The group around him shouted some more.

"Yeah, me too!" another guy yelled.

Clarissa was grinning along with them, the only girl in a sea of testosterone. She tossed her long, corkscrew curls over her shoulder. "Me too!"

My shoulders tensed. *You wish.* How dare she act so familiar about Leo. I wondered if she knew I was close by, listening.

The football guy let out a loud scoff. "No you don't!" I couldn't tell whether he was jealous or just doubtful.

"Yes I do!" Clarissa's whiny voice protested, and I strained to hear her words over the joking of the guys. "He even told me the other day that he was going to kill it when he batted cleanup!"

Every cell in my body went numb with a tingling sensation. What was Leo doing talking to Clarissa about the details of his baseball game? What was he doing talking to Clarissa at all? I pushed away a surge of tears, trying to figure it out—make it better. She had to be lying. It was completely and totally like her to make up something like that. Still, she sounded so confident— so casual and sincere about it. My pulse throbbed in every vein.

What if it was true? I played back Clarissa's words. *"He told me..."* My gut gripped at the thought of Leo talking to her, sharing something with her. *"...When he batted cleanup."* Batted cleanup? He hadn't even told me what that *was*—let alone the fact that he was excited about it.

The all-over tingling gave way to a shaking in my arms and legs as I tried to get a hold of my thoughts, but the rest of the game consisted of me waiting in agonized silence. More than anything, I wanted it to end so I could talk to Leo. He would fix it—reassure me that Clarissa was nothing but a liar.

As the last out was caught, the whole crowd stood,

cheering at our home-team win. Clive pointed down the stands as he leaned across Isaiah toward me. "Isn't that your dad?"

On one of the bleachers below, my dad was looking up toward us, staring. My already-thumping chest tightened even more. What in the world was he doing here? Was he just here to watch baseball, or was he checking on me? *Great.* This was the last thing I needed.

I leaned in close to Isaiah. "Tell Leo I had to go, okay?" I whispered. There was no way I could stay and see him after the game now. At this point, I was so twisted in knots that I wasn't even sure I wanted to see him. No. I did want to. I wanted to see him so he could reassure me, laugh with me... tell me that nothing Clarissa said was true.

Isaiah nodded with a frown, and I hated his pity as I forced a smile and headed toward my dad, stepping down the bleachers one by one.

"Hey, Dad." I stopped in front of him, summoning a carefree smile. "So, you felt like watching some baseball today?" He had his Cubs hat on, but he was still sporting his white work shirt with the button-down collar. I studied his face. He didn't seem suspicious or anything.

"I got out of the office early. Thought I'd come check it out." He motioned his head toward the field. "It was a good game."

The crowd steadily emptied out of the bleachers around us, and I dug around in my bag for my keys. A loud group of girls filed by, one of them bumping me as they passed. I scooted over to avoid the group and recognized the girl as Jude's friend from art class. "Hey Dove!" she shouted, waving. Was she being friendly or sarcastic? "Leo was amazing!"

My breath stopped. A sick feeling washed over me

as a look of confusion jumped onto my dad's face.

Jude shouldered her friend, giggling alongside her. "But was he amazing in Santa Barbara? *That's* the question," she murmured and then let out a burst of laughter.

I stood there frozen. This was it. I was so dead. My life was over. A rush of adrenaline flooded my head, making the sky spin.

"Why is she talking to you about Leo?" My dad frowned. His tone was confused, skeptical, maybe. Hadn't he heard Jude's Santa Barbara comment? If he had, he would have been livid—insane—beyond crazy. But Jude *had* sort of mumbled it. I studied his face, analyzing every inch of his expression as my heart raced. No. He hadn't heard it. But I still needed to fix this—fast. *Think.*

I gave him a nonchalant shrug. "I don't know," I answered, twisting my face like he was nuts or something. "We *are* still friends, Dad. Is that not okay?"

"Oh... right." His puzzled look began to melt into his normal doctor's poker face.

I rolled my eyes at him as though he had overreacted and tucked my hair behind my ear. I'd surprised myself with my slick reaction. Lying was starting to feel easier—smoother. I drove away the horrible idea. After all, this whole thing really was his fault. If he hadn't restricted me from seeing Leo, maybe I wouldn't have been desperate enough to hop on a stupid train. Forget *Roman Holiday*—hadn't he ever read *Romeo and Juliet*? Didn't he know that forbidding two people from seeing each other only makes them more desperate to be together?

One of my dad's friends passed down the aisle, stopping to talk to him, and I seized the opportunity to escape. "I'll see you at home." I waved, throwing my dad another reassuring smile.

As I headed toward my car, I stared out toward the tops of the windy Back Bay cliffs. Gusts of cool air blew my hair out in waves behind me. Had Juliet ever worried about some tramp making moves on Romeo? Or worse, had some tramp made Juliet doubt him? I wasn't an expert on Shakespeare, but I was pretty sure the answer was no.

Chapter 21

Breakfast at Tiffany's

I stretched out on my bed, my head propped on my pillow as I stared at the screen. Audrey was dancing with Humphrey in her white organdy *Sabrina* dress, its black embroidered flowers curling up and around her waist to the front of the gown. Humphrey stopped dancing just long enough to kiss her and then continued to move with her, cheek to cheek. I pointed the remote, fast-forwarding, and pushed the play button again at the sight of the two of them cruising along together in a sailboat as other boats in the harbor floated behind them in the distance.

My phone buzzed, but I ignored it, not wanting to break my trance and not wanting to think about what to say to Leo anymore. Almost the whole weekend had passed without seeing him, or really talking to him other than a few texts. He was busy Saturday with all of his baseball draft stuff, which worked out fine since my dad wanted me to stay in and study anyway. Besides, waiting to see him was a better idea. The last thing I wanted to be was some sort of whining, jealous girlfriend, and the longer I waited before I saw him, the calmer and more levelheaded I would be. My phone buzzed again. I finally rolled over to grab it.

Three unread messages from Leo glared at me, one after the other.

Can you get away today?

Dove? Today? Around 3?

Birdy where are you?

I sat up and started to type. *Sorry. They all just left for Laguna. Where do you want to go?*

I lay back on my pillow, wondering just how to go about bringing up the subject of Clarissa. My stomach clenched at the idea as her words played back in my head for the hundredth time: "*He told me.*" The buzz sounded again.

Great. Stay there. Gonna text in a minute.

Audrey tilted her head back, smiling at Humphrey. Sabrina wouldn't hesitate if she needed to say something. She'd just blurt it right out. I closed my eyes and collected myself. Yes. It really wasn't that complicated. I would just say it.

Humphrey leaned against the boat as it cut through the water, and I grabbed the remote, fast-forwarding again. That scene had always annoyed me. He should have kissed her out there on the water—it was obvious that he wanted to. My phone let out another buzz.

Look out your window.

I hopped off the bed and kneeled onto the cushion in the bay window, pushing back the curtain to peer out at the water. A small Boston Whaler sat idling at the dock in back of the house. Leo stood holding the wheel with one hand, waving up at me with the other. I flicked my eyes over him, taking in his shirtless, tan chest. Clive and Kai sat near him, waving at me from behind their sunglasses.

With my jaw dropped in surprise, I opened my window and leaned out. "Hey!"

"Get down here!" Leo grinned.

I tossed the remote onto the pile of homework on my desk, grabbed my flip-flops, and quickly high-fived Audrey's poster before I ran downstairs. The back door slammed as I trotted down the wooden planks to the end of the dock.

"Hey!" Leo reached out to help me into the boat. He leaned forward to kiss me, but I barely let my lips brush his before I sat on the white leathery chair beside him. He glanced at me sideways, questioning me with his squint, and I looked away, trying to summon every ounce of collectedness. *Let him wonder for a minute.*

He accelerated the boat, the engine roar blasting toward my house as the whaler sped across the bay.

"Bro, slow down." Clive moved toward us. "My dad will kill me if anything happens to his boat." Clive reached for the wheel, and I hopped up to give him my seat, edging toward the front of the little boat to sit next to Kai.

"Did you hear from any of the schools you applied to?" I asked, trying my best to ignore Leo.

Kai let out a breath and rolled her eyes. "No, not yet. Have you?"

I shook my head. "Jessie got two acceptance letters already, but I haven't heard anything."

"Well, it's only the first week of March. That's a little early still," she said, shrugging. "Are you going anywhere for spring break?"

"If I get accepted to the San Francisco Art Institute, my parents want to take me there to check it out... what about you?"

161

Her face lit up. "Clive and I are going to Hawaii with my mom."

I tried my best to look excited for her, but the thought of having parents who didn't disapprove of her relationship only made me jealous. Here she was, headed off on a weeklong trip with her boyfriend. I was dying to know what their sleeping arrangements would be, but I couldn't bring myself to ask.

I looked over at Leo, just to get a glimpse, but my eyes locked onto his. He was leaning against the back of the chair, his eyes fixed on me. His chest rose and fell with each breath. How long had he been sitting there, staring? He didn't let go of me with his gaze. Clearly, he wanted to know why I'd dodged his kiss. The half of me that believed Clarissa's story had an urge to slap his smug face. But the other half wished he would just come over and try to kiss me again, because this time I wouldn't be able to resist.

He stood from his chair, and I moved my gaze to the homes on the waterfront in the distance, readying myself. Without leaving even an inch of space between us, he sat down next to me on the edge of the boat, not saying a word. I waited.

"Why didn't you want to kiss me?" he finally asked.

Okay. The straightforward route. Sounded good to me. Kai stood, flashing me a look, and scooted away toward Clive. Now was the time. My pulse quickened. "Friday at the game, I heard Clarissa going on about how she knows you, and she said you were talking to her about baseball."

His nostrils flared, and he bit his lips together as he slowly nodded. "Why didn't you just tell me this?" he asked, now shaking his head. "I've been wondering what was up with you all weekend."

I looked down at my flip-flops, moving them with my toes. "I didn't want to act like a jealous girlfriend or something. I knew she was probably lying..." Leo leaned toward me. His brow wrinkled as I looked up at him, setting my jaw. "Was she lying?"

He shook his head no, and I bit the inside of my cheek. *No?* My mind raced. *No, she was lying, or no, she wasn't lying?*

His eyes rolled in a circle, and he cracked a smile as he looked out at the water and then back to me. "I was walking out of the weight room the other day, and she was just standing there... I don't know if she was waiting for me or what..."

Of course she was. Why were guys so clueless?

"...So she starts walking with me and asking me all these questions about baseball, and I was just, you know, trying to answer her and get to my truck as fast as possible so I could get the hell out of there."

Relief rippled through me. He reached out to grab my hand. "I wish you would've just asked me about it when it happened."

I raised my eyebrows in a silent apology and pursed my lips into a smile as I pulled him to me. He moved closer, sliding one hand onto my back and the other behind my head as he pulled me onto his lap. At first his lips only skimmed mine, then with sudden intensity he pressed harder, exploring my mouth with his. I melted into his grip as the strength of his arm grabbed me to him, his fingers clutching the back of my neck. He finally broke away, breathing heavily, pressing his forehead against mine. My eyes darted out to the water as a sailboat glided past in the other direction. A smile crept onto my face. That was it. The kiss I'd always wanted Humphrey to give Audrey on the boat. I had just lived it.

Chapter 22

Breakfast at Tiffany's

I peered out my kitchen window for the tenth time. A few younger kids began to trickle onto the street and sidewalk in the after-school hours, their sounds of laughter and shouting carrying in from outside. With my phone wedged between my chin and shoulder, I tapped my finger impatiently on the windowsill. Jessie answered on the other end.

"Did your mail come yet?" I blurted.

"Hello to you, too." She laughed. "I don't think so—she hasn't been delivering till around four lately."

I forced out a breath. "I don't get why I haven't heard from San Francisco yet."

"Did you check your email?"

"Obsessively."

Jessie let out a tiny groan from her end. "Maybe you need to practice Zen breathing or something."

"Easy for you to say. You're a rock star. Vassar, NYU,

164

and Boston College."

"Yeah, but—"

"No." I stopped her short. "Don't even start about how you haven't heard from Harvard yet. I'm still waiting for two letters."

Two acceptance letters had finally arrived, one from Savannah and one from Chicago, and all of a sudden moving to Georgia or Illinois seemed like moving to another planet. How had I gotten myself in this deep? Unfortunately, now my dad was over-the-top elated about Chicago, and I'd have to really rely on Patty to help me convince him that San Francisco would be a better choice. But, first, I had to actually get into San Francisco.

"It's just ridiculous that your dad didn't want you to apply to the East Coast." Jessie's voice was muffled by some kind of chewing. "I mean, we could have ended up in New York together—like painting the town red, or whatever that saying is."

"Yeah." I paused. The thought of going in different directions sent out a pang of sadness, leaving only Jessie's smacking sounds to fill the silence. "What are you eating?"

"Chocolate kisses," she mumbled.

"That's it, I'm coming over," I said before shoving my phone into my back pocket. I headed out the front door and crossed the lawn. Down the street, the sound of an idling engine stopped me. I stood still, watching the mail truck stop two houses away, then one. There was no way to escape the childlike embarrassment that crept up as I stood there waiting next to my black mailbox. The white truck pulled forward to a stop, and the friendly face of our mail carrier peeked out the open window.

165

"Hey Janice," I said, giving her an awkward wave.

Janice bent toward me, filling my arms with a big stack of envelopes and catalogues. "Expecting something today?"

"Yeah, hoping."

"Well, good luck." She winked as she leaned back to her steering wheel and guided the little truck forward to the next house.

I shifted the pile of mail in my arms and began to flip through, searching out the larger envelopes. The whole college correspondence thing was pretty straightforward. A big envelope was always a yes, and a thin, smaller letter meant a brief but polite rejection.

I spied a large white envelope in the middle of the pile and quickly grabbed for it. *Parsons Paris* stared at me from the upper left-hand corner. A ripple of excitement coursed through me as my gaze dropped to the word *Congratulations* printed across the bottom.

I stared at the huge black lettering, trying to take it in. Parsons had accepted me. I was in. I took a breath as a myriad of confusion raced through my brain. What exactly was inside? Had I received the scholarship I'd been trying to win for the last two years? And if they did give me the scholarship, what was the point of all that work to then just turn it down?

I tucked the envelope under my arm, part of me almost wishing there would be no scholarship inside. No scholarship would prove that Paris was never meant to be in the first place. I bit the inside of my cheek and began searching through the stack of mail again.

I continued to flip through the pile, my hopes plummeting at the absence of any more large envelopes. As I neared the bottom of the stack, my stomach jumped when my eyes fell upon the return address on the last piece of mail. *San Francisco Art Institute.* I turned it in my hand, studying it. It wasn't a large envelope, but it wasn't standard letter size, either. The squat, square shape was medium-sized and somewhat thick.

I stood staring at it for a moment, feeling as though a top-secret answer to my future was hidden behind the plain, white wrapping. Then again, it could be just another one of their standard informational brochures. I took a deep breath. There was no way to know without opening it.

I shoved the excess mail into the mailbox and then made my way down the block with my two envelopes in hand, still examining the smaller one. If a rejection was inside, then that would be it. There would be no chance of ending up near Leo unless some sort of miracle happened. What then? Would we be forced to go our separate ways, no matter how we felt about each other? I pictured Audrey, her back turned to Gregory Peck as she walked away from him down the long, marble hallway. Princess Ann and Joe Bradley couldn't be together. It was the way it had to be. And it was the reason I cried my eyes out every single time at the end of *Roman Holiday.*

As I rounded the corner to Jessie's, something caught my eye in the distance. On the curb in front of her house, Jessie sat hunched over, her head buried in her arms. At the sight, I started to run. "Jessie? Are you okay? What is it?"

She lifted her head. Strands of hair fell messy and tangled over her tear-stained face. A surge of emotion overtook her, twisting her expression, and she lowered her head back to her knees. With her face still down, she lifted a small envelope into the air. *Harvard* was printed in the corner, and the flap had been ripped open.

I took the letter with one hand and sat down on the curb to wrap my arm around her.

She sniffed and brushed the hair out of her eyes. "At least they were nice enough to say that my rejection is not necessarily a true indicator of my future success or potential."

"Well, that's for sure."

"It could be worse." She sniffed again.

"Uh, it could be a lot worse. Three amazing schools accepted you, Jess, and competition for Ivy League schools is insane. Besides, you're going to go there for law school later on. You don't want to be sick of it by then." I nudged her with my shoulder. "Right? Jessie Walsh, Esquire?"

Jessie laughed and sniffed at the same time. "I need more chocolate." She lifted her head and looked at me, eyeing my envelopes. "Whoa!" She grabbed at the big one as her eyes widened. "Yes from Parsons? Oh my God, you did it!"

I let a grin escape but then shook my head, slowing her down. "But I don't know about the scholarship yet—not that it really matters."

She frowned, pointing to the other letter. "What's that one?"

I held it up to her, letting her examine it. "Good question. I have no idea what's in there. I think I'll need some chocolate, too."

Inside, I laid the envelopes side by side on the coffee table. Jessie wedged in next to me on the couch and stared with me at the two letters, her sniffs less frequent now. She ran her fingers through her hair, attempting to smooth it to one side. The foil-covered Hershey's Kisses had spilled out of the bag onto the coffee table, and I unwrapped one before chewing it in silence.

I turned to Jessie, studying her huge brown eyes and pretty mess of auburn hair. My stomach twisted as I fought back a surge of tears. Somehow, this beautiful person had gotten lost in the craziness of college applications and the senior year shuffle of my life. I bit the inside of my cheek, weighing the idea. No—if I was going to be honest with myself, I had to admit that she had gotten lost in the shuffle of *Leo* in my life.

I pulled my knees up onto the couch. "Hold on. Before I open these—I want to talk to you. There's something I've been meaning to tell you about Isaiah."

"Okay," she said, frowning. And, for a second, I reconsidered. Maybe now wasn't the time to tell her when she was feeling so upset. On the flip side, maybe it was the perfect time.

"I just... I got the feeling the other day at the baseball game that he missed you."

She grabbed a piece of chocolate and began unwrapping it. "Why?"

"Well..." I hesitated, not knowing exactly how to convince her. "He asked where you were, and he seemed really... interested."

"That's it?" She rolled her eyes at me. "He was probably just being friendly."

I squinted, shaking my head. "I don't think so—"

"It's just your wishful thinking," she said, dismissing me. "Stop stalling. Which one first?" she asked, moving her eyes back and forth from one envelope to the other.

I frowned at her but didn't answer right away. Staring at the letters again, I savored the chocolate while I contemplated the two. The thought of no news or bad news from San Francisco was enough to put it off, even if only for a couple more minutes. "Let's just see what Parsons said first."

169

A thick, red folder was tucked neatly underneath the formal acceptance letter when I pulled the contents from the package. Slowly, I opened the folder, my gaze falling on the detailed columns of scholarship offerings. At the top of the columns, bright red letters announced a full merit scholarship for the fall and spring semesters. I closed my eyes. I had actually done it. Aunt Gail would not believe it.

"Woooow." Jessie leaned into me. "You got it?" She eyed my shocked expression and then leaned in again to study the paper. "You got it!" She shook her head at me, letting out a laugh. "Ooooh, your dad's gonna hate this."

"It's pretty amazing." I smiled, admiring the red folder again. "I guess Aunt Gail was right. My portfolio must be better than I realized."

Jessie shot me a proud, I-told-you-so smile, then pushed the square envelope closer to me. "Okay... next."

I stared at the odd-shaped letter for a moment before reaching out to grab it. As soon as I picked up the envelope, nervousness overtook my fumbling fingers. I shoved it at Jessie. "You do it."

Without hesitating, Jessie tore it open, pulled out the letter and unfolded four large flaps to reveal an artsy, colorful announcement. "*Congratulations on your admission to the San Francisco School of Art and Design,*" she read aloud.

I grabbed the pretty letter to read the large, printed words for myself and then clasped it to my chest. Falling back onto the soft cushions, I blinked at the ceiling, smiling.

The abstract painting hanging on the wall above us caught my eye, and I turned my head to take it in. That first night when Leo was here, it had been propped up in the garage. I stared at the crazy splatter of orange in the corner. It was the whole reason I'd hit my nose. The reason he came to help me. All of a sudden, I loved that stupid splash of orange more than anything. I sat forward, hugging Jessie.

"That's four yeses. Now who's the rock star?" Jessie asked, squeezing me tightly.

"This means I'm San Francisco bound for spring break!" I grinned. "And it's perfect timing before the Bayport art show, too. I told Ms. Atkins I'd help with the display. I'll get some good ideas there."

"Senior year and you're spending spring break with your family." Jessie let out a sigh. "That's just wrong."

I frowned at the prospect of letting Jessie down again. "I'm so sorry. I have to do it to convince my dad—but I'll really miss you, Jess."

"Nah." Jessie shrugged away my look of concern. "Don't worry about it." She smiled. "The nice thing is, you won't need to work very hard at convincing your dad about San Francisco. Patty will do the work for you." She raised her eyebrows and smirked. "And we know how persuasive she can be with him, especially when she's sporting her spandex."

I rolled my eyes and let out a chuckle. "I hope you're right." I grabbed another chocolate piece, unwrapping it. "And then there will be only one last thing to worry about."

"What's that?" Jessie's eyebrows arched again. "Figuring out where to park your car in San Francisco?"

"No." I drew in a slow breath. "MLB draft day," I said before popping the chocolate into my mouth.

The plastic bag of chocolates crinkled as Jessie clutched it with one hand and dragged it across the coffee table toward her. "These are mine, by the way. Let's not forget that."

Chapter 23

 "Do you really want to see me?"
-Sabrina Fairchild

Sabrina

I waited as Leo's phone rang on the other end once, twice, then three times. His voicemail finally picked up. *"Hey it's Leo, leave a message."*

"Hi, it's me," I breathed. "I'm back. I texted you a million times. I can't wait to see you. Call me, okay?"

The news was too good to let him know over the phone. I couldn't wait to see the look on his face when I told him it was one-hundred-percent official. I'd be going to the San Francisco Art Institute in September. I grabbed my coat and headed out back to the dock, walking barefoot through the darkness across the damp, wooden boards to my favorite perch on the edge.

Spending spring break in San Francisco with my dad and Patty had been completely worth it. We'd toured the college and visited every interesting spot in the city. My dad needed less convincing than I thought he would, thanks in part to Patty, and to the fact that being in San Francisco meant that I would be close enough to visit more often.

The tide was high in the harbor, and I touched the tips of my toes into the water, wondering how long I should wait before calling Leo again. Glancing at the storage chest, I considered the idea of pulling out a drawing pad when "Moon River" rang out from my phone, interrupting the thought. *There* he was. I grabbed it from my pocket.

"Hey," Leo's voice echoed.

"Hi... I have something to tell you," I blurted.

"Really?" His voice sounded low—depressed almost.

"What's wrong?" My burst of energy screeched to a stop. "Are you okay?"

"Yeah, I'm okay, I'm just... it's my dad. He went to New York today, but we kinda got in an argument about all the draft stuff before he left. I'm okay, though. How was your trip? What did you want to tell me?"

"Oh. Well, I want to see you first. Should I come over?"

"I don't think you can, really." He sighed. "They're doing tons of construction tonight on Pacific Coast Highway. The peninsula is all blocked off near Newport Boulevard and the bridge. The traffic's crazy. We'll have to wait till tomorrow."

Disappointment sank into my chest. "Oh, right." I sat thinking on my end of the phone, but he didn't fill the silence. "Okay," I finally spoke up. "Well, I hope you're okay."

"Don't worry, I'm fine." He didn't sound fine. "I'm not very good company right now, anyway. Wanna grab breakfast at Angelo's tomorrow?"

"Sure," I answered, trying to sound cheerful. Sunday breakfast out wasn't half as appealing as Saturday dinner in. Especially when his dad was out of town.

We picked a time to meet, and hung up, leaving me

staring out at the docked boats across the bay. Water lapped against them as a small cruiser chugged past in the darkness.

The ferry. The thought dawned on me, and I didn't even need to think about it. It was perfect. The Balboa Ferry would drop me off in the center of the peninsula, circumventing all the construction. No doubt it would be open on Saturday night. I jumped up and ran inside, changing into my favorite blue sweater, remembering when Leo had said he loved it because it matched my eyes. After a whole week apart, I wouldn't have to wait any longer for my eyes to meet his.

WITH THE COLD OF the night forcing me to leave the top up, I drove across the bridge to Balboa Island and waited in the line of cars at the landing. A ferryboat loaded up the three cars in front of me and took off into the bay, its lights shining out across the darkness. A second ferry docked in the landing and raised its large metal railing, its three cars unloading to drive past me onto the island. The attendant waved, motioning me forward, and the large wooden ramp creaked under the weight as I drove down it and pulled up to the front of the ferry. Two more cars drove in behind me as several people and bicyclists boarded, too, sitting down on the benches along the sides of the boat.

A breeze blew over the choppy water. It was the end of spring break, but it was impossible to know it by looking around. The unexpected cold weather had everyone wrapped in jackets and sweaters, huddling together for the short ride across the bay.

When the ferryboat bumped up against the landing,

I drove under the lifted railing and up the planks onto the peninsula. A feverish thrill fluttered through me. My spontaneous idea was pretty clever and romantic. Definitely worthy of an Audrey stamp of approval.

I pulled up in front of the condo and opened my car door, shivering when the foggy night air rushed in, gripping me with its chill. Grabbing my wool beanie, I tugged it onto my head and held my coat tight over my sweater as I jogged up the steps to ring the doorbell. My stomach flipped when Leo's footsteps thudded down the stairs, and then the door swung open.

He stood in front of me wearing jeans and no shirt, looking sexy as ever.

"Dove!" My surprise had worked. His eyebrows flew up, but he still seemed sad somehow, which made me all the more sure about my decision to come over.

"I'm here to cheer you up." I shot him a mischievous smile and stepped into the front hallway, leaning into him. His kiss was guarded, and he didn't grab me into his arms like usual. This baseball thing was more serious than I had realized. *His dad must've really been a jerk.* I reached up to brush the hair out of his eyes. "Are you okay?"

"Leo?" a soft voice called out from above. I turned to see the silhouette of a girl standing at the top of the stairs. Blonde ringlets cascaded over her shoulders.

Clarissa.

Her long, perfect legs peeked out from underneath the only piece of clothing she was wearing: Leo's red Angels jersey.

Chapter 24

"You mustn't give your heart to a wild thing."
-Holly Golightly

Breakfast at Tiffany's

I backed away from Leo, my hands fumbling for the door. Horror mixed with humiliation inside my suddenly spinning head. Stepping sideways out the front doorway, my eyes shot from Clarissa to Leo and back again. They both stood frozen, Clarissa's face stony yet triumphant. Leo stared at the ground, unwilling to bring his eyes to meet mine.

Somehow my body guided me out the front door and to my car, and when I pulled to a stop in front of my own house, I couldn't remember any details of the ride home. It was as if the shock had caused my brain to shift into its own version of autopilot, taking over in crisis mode and steering me home.

I stepped into the house without hiding my puffy eyes, too preoccupied with the image of Clarissa to even think about making myself presentable. It seemed impossible to find the strength to care about what my dad or Patty might ask. Thankfully, it was just Griffin who walked out of the family room to greet me in the hallway.

"What's wrong?" His little face frowned.

More tears welled. I gulped back the sound in my throat, trying not to sob in his presence. "Nothing, Griffy," was all I could manage. I took the stairs up two at a time and shut the door to my room.

Diving into my bed without bothering to undress, I pulled the blankets over my head and tried to escape the swirling thoughts of Leo. Nothing could have prepared me for a half-naked Clarissa standing in his living room. The sobs came, now unstoppable, heaving and surging from someplace deep inside. There was no escape from the horrific reality.

The look on Clarissa's face flashed in my mind, then the memory of Leo. His guarded kiss—his excuses for not seeing me that night. All lies. I thought back over the past eight months. Had all of it been a lie? Instinct told me no, but I had no idea what to believe now.

The image of Piper floated toward me menacingly. I had ignored her warning. I'd fallen back on the idea that her relationship with Leo was a short, little fling— it didn't compare. But now, curled up in a ball and sobbing uncontrollably, I realized it didn't matter. Piper predicted he would break my heart, and she was right. I buried my head deeper into my pillow. This time I was a fool for sure.

SUNDAY MORNING PATTY SUSPECTED nothing when, under the guise of the stomach flu, I didn't emerge from my bed—the idea of omelets unthinkable.

I closed my eyes and tried to breathe away the

darkness. Idealistic. That's what I had been. How could I possibly have thought that our love was synonymous to some old Hollywood romance? How many times had I compared our relationship to Audrey and Humphrey, or Audrey and Gregory Peck? Too many.

Leo never acted like he expected me to sleep with him. He'd never pushed it or anything. Beyond his occasional suggestion of *someday*, we hadn't really talked about it a whole lot. Tears surged, and I reached up to cover my face even though I was alone. Apparently, the whole sex thing was a bigger issue than I realized. Perhaps I'd been stupid to think that a guy with a playboy reputation would slow to a screeching halt. Still, this didn't come down to just sex, did it? I took a deep breath. No. Not for me, at least. It came down to honesty. Trust.

I tortured myself, going over it all in my head, attempting to figure out just where I went wrong. How long had I believed his lies? And did those lies mean our love was a lie? Deep down, something tried to remind me that what we had was real. The thought briefly comforted me, and then turned into sheer torment. Because despite that fact, I would not—and could not— be with him anymore.

I propped myself upright in bed and looked over at my phone, wondering just how many more messages he'd left for me since I turned it off the night before. It didn't matter. There would be no excuses this time.

THE NEXT MORNING, JESSIE offered to drive to school together in her Jeep, and I agreed, glad for the refuge of her company. The entire senior class had probably heard at least some version of the story, but it was time to face all of them... including Leo. A few wisps of hair not caught up into my ponytail whipped across my face as we rode along in silence.

"You cold? You want the heater?" Jessie had managed to make it through the California winter without ever putting the top back on the Jeep.

"No, thanks."

She waited for several more minutes before she spoke again. "Did you talk to him?"

"No." I surprised myself at the coldness in my own voice. "He left more messages, though. Just the same stuff, going on about how she followed him around all of spring break and how he finally just caved, how he's so sorry—on and on like that."

The truth was that I almost believed him—in fact, I *did* believe him. But I also knew that none of it mattered anymore. I'd been naïve. It was time to be more mature about life and love and whatever the hell else might happen to pop up unexpectedly. The Jeep turned into the crowded school parking lot, curving around to a stop.

Bring it on. I bolstered myself with the thought and climbed out with as much courage as I could muster.

Chapter 25

"TRUE. ABSOLUTELY TRUE. TRUE, BUT IRRELEVANT."
-HOLLY GOLIGHTLY

Breakfast at Tiffany's

Setting up for Bayport High's art show was a good distraction now that my weekend afternoons and evenings were completely empty. The sick feeling in my stomach hadn't stopped its plaguing for two whole weeks, though I tried to divert my attention from the thought of Leo in more ways than one. Ignoring his presence everyday during English class had become a predictable routine, and Leo seemed to catch on, almost making it easier for me by sitting as far away as possible.

I immersed myself in work at the gallery every day after school, and there were a couple of times when I almost forgot about him. But soon enough, a little nagging sensation would crawl forward from the back of my mind, and I would remember my shattered heart again.

Friday afternoon, the art room looked better than I had ever seen it, and it wasn't even finished yet. Aunt Gail had loaned the school an assortment of easels and frames, and I threw myself into the job of display. A bunch of other art students showed up to help, and as crazed as ever, Ms. Atkins ordered everyone around in her friendly, flustered way.

I turned from the hallway into the supply room, caught up in the thought of a frameless acrylic. A breeze blew through the wide-open utility door, and I stopped and stared. On the back steps stood Leo.

Glancing away, I searched the room for the thin black frame I had come for, but everything was a blur. It was impossible to concentrate. Leo stepped up and leaned against the large, open doorway. I finally turned to him.

"Hey, Birdy," he said quietly.

Tears welled up, but I refused to let them surface, forcing myself to search again for the black frame. "Please don't do this, Leo. Don't make it more difficult. We've already decided." I stepped around an old easel, flipping through the stacks of artwork and supplies.

He didn't move. "You decided it. Not me."

Did he really have the nerve to sound bitter? I spun around to face him. "Uh, no. I think when you slept with Clarissa you made your decision."

"Dove, please, I'm so sorry. I'm so, *so* sorry. What can I do? *Please*, forgive me. Please..." His final plea choked in his throat.

Sadness washed back over my anger. I couldn't stop the tears now. "Please, Leo, there's nothing we can do about it."

"Dove, *why*?" His voice was desperate. "I know you feel it. We have something special. It's—I don't know—a connection to each other."

I understood exactly what he meant, but I pushed it away, brushing the tears from my cheeks. "It doesn't matter what I feel anymore, Leo, it matters what I think." My voice slowed. "And... I can't do it."

More than anything, I wanted his arms to wrap around me, to lean against him and go back to those times when it had only been the two of us. But like magic it had come, and like magic it had disappeared. Time had caught up with us. Real life would have to be lived now. I stared into his deep brown eyes. Why was it so hard to hurt him, even though he had torn my heart up into little pieces? That shredded heart was arguing with my head. I had to follow my head this time. Maybe if I reasoned with him, he could face it.

"It's not just... Clarissa." My stomach turned when I said her name, but I forced myself to keep going. "It's my dad, it's graduating—and college. We're really young still. I don't want to be with anyone else... I just think I need to be alone now. I need to figure my life out and sort through everything." It sounded so cliché. But now I knew why people said it. It was true, like a horrible paradox of life, or some universal truth of growing up.

A few students rounded the corner into the supply room and Leo quieted his voice to almost a whisper. "Don't do this, Dove. You don't need to be alone. You need me, and I need you. Don't throw it away." He stepped backward through the open doorway and down the steps, waiting for one last opportunity to lock his gaze with mine.

I forced my eyes to face his as I clenched my jaw, refusing to give in to his magnetic pull. "I didn't throw it away, Leo. You did."

Chapter 26

> "But, I'm trying to get over it."
> -Sabrina Fairchild

Sabrina

The door to the gallery clicked shut when Saturday afternoon came to an end. Aunt Gail turned the key in the lock and reached over to prop up the closed sign.

Sitting at the front desk, I leaned my head on my hand and stared out the front window. My aunt sat down on a chair in front of the desk and tilted her head back, eyeing me. "How did it go at the art show last night?"

"Fine, except for the fact that Leo showed up before it even started," I said, leaning all the way forward to rest my forehead on the shiny wood.

"You know, your dad has no idea what's going on with you, and Patty keeps trying to convince him you're depressed."

I didn't lift my head. "She's right."

My aunt grabbed a pile of papers from the desk and began to flip through it. "You need to get your mind off everything."

183

"I don't think that's possible," I mumbled.

"Yes it is." She slid two tickets under my nose.

I lifted my head, brushing the hair out of my eyes to get a better look. "*Love's Labour's Lost* by William Shakespeare?" I flashed her a look. "A play about love is supposed to get my mind off it?"

"Mmhmm." She nodded. "Going to the theater transports you to another world. You're going to love it. It might help you see things from a new perspective."

I laid my forehead back onto the desk, my hair falling around my face again. "You know, your Audrey optimism used to inspire me, but now I'm finding it pretty annoying."

I stared at the grainy wood in front of my eyes. Had I just used *Audrey* and *annoying* in the same sentence? Not okay. I lifted my head and then my chin as I smoothed my hair into place. "Sorry... never mind." I blinked my eyelids deliberately, summoning my forgotten dignity. "You're right. Let's do it."

AUNT GAIL AND I weaved across the crowded plaza to the entrance of the Performing Arts Center and entered the huge foyer, passing beneath its massive lighted sculpture hanging from above. For a moment, my sadness almost vanished in the midst of the bustle and excitement of the crowded lobby, but one glance at the sweeping staircase leading to the balcony was enough to remind me of Clarissa at the top of Leo's stairway, and the heavy gloom returned. It was no use. Everything reminded me of him.

Inside the theater, we made our way to the tenth row and took our seats on the aisle. Lengths of white taffeta painted with ornate, leafy trees decorated the empty stage. A hush finally settled over the crowd when four actors stepped onto the platform, talking back and forth in loud voices.

One of the actors walked further down the stage in his brown boots and cape. He tossed his blond hair as he turned and shouted out his lines, giving off nothing but poise.

I leaned forward as my eyes widened. It was... it was... what was his name? *Henry.* From the fair. The guy who had bumped into me.

I sat back against the red velvet chair, thumbing through my program in the darkness. There, on one of the glossy pages, his picture stared back at me. *Henry Kentworthy as Berowne* was printed below the photo, along with descriptions of his acting credits from theaters all over Britain.

The group of actors had complete command over the audience now, with alternating laughter and silence filling the packed theater. I continued to follow Henry's movements, watching him carefully even when the spotlight shined somewhere else on the stage. Every one of his actions was self-assured and purposeful. Where did all of that confidence come from?

Further along into the play, he sat down on a platform, put his elbow on his knee, and looked up. Elaborate phrases fell out of his mouth with complete ease as he spoke on and on about Rosaline, the girl he loved. From the vantage point of only ten rows away, I watched every expression on his face as his speech continued in perfect cadence. His willingness to be so vulnerable mesmerized me as I let myself be caught up in the moment, gazing at him in admiration as his British accent lilted on, the words still spilling out.

All of a sudden, his eyes, wandering the audience as he spoke, stopped at mine. I shifted in my seat and tried to dismiss it as nothing. There could be no way he really saw me—or recognized me, for that matter. But his eyes stayed locked onto mine while the words of love intended for Rosaline flowed into me. It was all gibberish now. Beautiful, melodious gibberish. He stood and walked down the stage, never moving his stare from mine, and tenseness gripped me as my heart began to beat faster. I straightened my shoulders and pulled my gaze from his, my eyes darting around the stage looking for a place to land.

When I found the courage to look at him again, his shoulder was turned toward another actor. But as the play continued on, his eyes rested on mine each time he had a reason to turn in my direction. I began to second-guess myself. Was I deluded or something? There was no way this guy actually recognized me all the way out in the audience. I had to be imagining his attention in my needy, brokenhearted state.

The play ended to tons of applause, with the whole company stepping forward in their extravagant costumes to bow together as the lights went up. I didn't move my eyes from Henry as he bowed over and again, caught up along with the rest of the troupe in the applause of the crowd. He glanced once more in my direction before he turned and left through a carved wooden door at the back of the stage.

The entire platform stood quiet now, empty of actors. Aunt Gail stood to go and I followed, shooting one more look at the vacant stage. It *had* been a great story, and Aunt Gail was right, escaping into another world was the perfect way to spend my evening.

As we edged through the crowded lobby, I steered

my aunt toward a souvenir cart. T-shirts with the Globe Theatre logo were stacked in piles on the shelves with little knickknacks lined above them. My mom had always loved to collect little keepsakes from special places we went together. Remembrances, she called them. A remembrance seemed like a good idea tonight. A little something from a historic, British landmark to remind me that someday I'd go to Europe and visit all the great places I'd only ever seen in movies. Maybe I would even paint the Globe Theatre someday. I clutched onto the bag that held my small purchase—a tiny snow globe with the round, thatched-roof theater inside it— and we fell again into the flow of people moving toward the huge doorway.

I blinked three times. Up ahead, only twenty feet away, Henry was walking against the flow of the crowd, dressed only in jeans and a white T-shirt. A zing of excitement jumped into my chest, making it pound. Without his fancy costume, no one else in the crowded lobby seemed to recognize him. He was turning his head this way and that, like he was searching for something.

I stopped in my tracks. Was he looking for *me*? It wasn't possible, was it? *Don't flatter yourself, Dove,* I scolded myself as we continued to walk toward the large doorway. Ten feet away now, I could see the details of his face—his light blue eyes, his blond hair, the way his mouth curved upward in an almost-smile, even though his brow wrinkled in thought.

I couldn't move my eyes from him as he came closer. He continued to look as though he were searching through the crowd until, only a few feet away, his gaze finally landed on me. His eyebrows shot to the ceiling and he reached out, almost touching my arm, but then stopped himself. "Hello!" he breathed.

187

My eyes flew wide open as my stare broke into a smile. "Hi!"

His face lit up as he grinned. "It's Dove, isn't it? Do you remember me? I recognized you in the audience!" His English accent tumbled out fast.

"Yes! You're Henry. I... tripped you at the fair last summer." Warmth began to tingle into my cheeks.

"It was the best trip I ever took," he joked, his eyes now dancing with mischief.

My grin grew wider. He actually came to find me in the lobby. He *was* staring at me the entire play. I turned and introduced him to my aunt, then complimented him on his performance, but he shrugged it away with another charming smile.

As the crowd milled around us, he pulled his phone from his jeans pocket. "I hope you don't think this presumptuous of me, but may I give you my phone number?" The question lilted upward in his British way. "I'm here for two more weeks, and I'd love to see you again. Perhaps you might give me your number, as well?"

I stared at him for a moment, my head rushing with thoughts. Should I? Leo's face flashed in my mind. Strangely, it felt wrong to even be talking to another guy. But in light of everything, a date with Henry might be a good thing.

"Yes, I'd love that." I glanced over at my aunt, who just stood there with a polite smile. Her eyes glinted though, teasing me almost. I fumbled for my phone and quickly typed Henry's number in, then added his name.

"Okay." I looked up at him. "And I just sent you mine."

He glanced down at his phone as it dinged. "Dove." He nodded at the phone and then at me, his blue eyes sparkling. "Lovely to see you again."

Chapter 27

Angelo set the warm plates in front of Jessie and me and then winked without any of his usual loud conversation. Ever since I'd told him about the breakup, he'd made a sweet, obvious effort to tiptoe around me. I stared at the back of his apron as he headed toward the kitchen. Jessie dug into her breakfast, and I stabbed at my own scrambled eggs, finally hungry for the first time in two weeks.

"I can't believe he came to find you in the lobby. That's crazy." Jessie shook her head at her omelet.

"What's crazy is the idea of dating someone else." I shrugged. "I mean, it's only been a couple of weeks."

"Weeks, shmeeks." Jessie waved her fork in the air. "This is good for you. You don't owe Leo *anything*."

I rubbed my forehead at the sound of Leo's name. "What about you? Have you talked to Isaiah lately?" I raised my eyebrows at her, unwilling to hide my position on the matter anymore. Having my love shatter to

189

pieces was enough reason to push her to fight for what she wanted.

"No, Dovey, I haven't." She shot me an irritated glance before rolling her eyes.

My phone rang beside my plate and I glanced down at the screen. "It's him," I said, unblinking.

"Who?"

"Henry!"

Her eyebrows flew up. "Answer it!"

"Hi, Henry." I looked out the window toward the boats in the harbor to avoid being distracted by the comical look on Jessie's face.

"Hello, Dove." There was that charming accent again.

Jessie grinned and sipped her orange juice. "He didn't waste any time!" she whispered.

I smiled and looked down at the glossy tabletop, trying to concentrate on Henry's voice.

"May I take you to dinner this week? I can't do the weekend with the show and all, but Thursday, perhaps?"

I cupped my hand against the phone, shielding it from my whisper. "He wants to take me to dinner!"

Jessie did a mini dance in her seat.

"Thursday sounds great," I answered, smiling.

Henry continued on, making the interesting small talk he was so good at doing as we made our plans. When I hung up, I set my phone on the table and looked up, unsure. What was I doing? I had just happily arranged a date for myself.

Jessie scowled at me, shaking her head. "This is completely okay, Dove. Would you stop guilt-tripping yourself?"

"It just feels weird, you know? Like I'm doing something wrong."

"Well you're not, so cut it out." She leaned in. "Okay,

tell me what the plan is."

"He's borrowing a friend's car to take me to dinner." I shrugged, ignoring the wave of excitement that coursed through me. "That's all."

Jessie rested her head back against the smooth, red booth. "I think I might have to strategically come over for a visit on Thursday night. I need to meet this guy."

THE NEXT WEEK APART from Leo proved to be no easier than the first two had been. The discomfort of art class with Clarissa was almost as bad as English class, where sitting in the same room with Leo for an hour everyday had become pure torture. Leo didn't look up from his desk very often, but when he did, he seemed to always glance in my direction, and I would pretend not to notice. His hunched shoulders and constant frown made my heart ache, and I found myself asking him *why* more than once from inside my head. Missing him had created a void, a darkness, which his presence always made worse. And arguing with myself about it had become a part of my daily routine. Should I reach out? Have mercy? Forgive him? But the reality of what he had done, and the memory of it, stopped me every time.

He made it halfway through the week without saying anything to me, until Wednesday after class, when he stood waiting in the hallway. As I walked through the classroom doorway, he stepped toward me.

"Dove, I was hoping—I was thinking—maybe you could come to my game tomorrow night?" He grabbed his neck, shrugging at me. "The scout from San Francisco is going to be there, and it's a really big game. I'd like it if you were there. Just… as friends."

Right. As friends. Way too much water had gone under the bridge for that. We would never be able to be just friends—he must know that. My heart ripped a little more at the look on his face when I shook my head. "I can't. I'm sorry, Leo. I have plans already."

Tomorrow was Thursday. I would be out with Henry when Leo wanted me at his game. As I walked away, a sick feeling crawled into my stomach, and I tried my best to chase it away with the thought that he had done this to himself entirely.

THURSDAY NIGHT, JESSIE WAS hanging out in the living room alongside my family when Henry arrived. Her boisterous jokes were the perfect antidote to the standard awkward introductions, and one look at the grin on my dad's face was enough to tell me that Henry had passed his test with flying colors. That same easy way Henry held himself on the stage transferred without effort to our living room. His relaxed conversation lilted with his charming accent, and by the time we headed out the doorway, everyone was nodding and laughing. Jessie shot me a toothy grin behind his back, pointing her thumbs up in the air. Not surprisingly, Henry's approval rating was a perfect ten.

We pulled away from the curb in his borrowed car, and he turned toward me with a smirk. "I really should have asked you to drive. This business of driving on the opposite side of the road is a bit tricky." He laughed. "I'll try to get you home in one piece."

"Just take it slow." I smiled.

"Yes, I'll try. So, where to? Where would a Newport girl take a London boy to show him the town? Perhaps someplace beachy, with seafood?"

I thought about it for a second. "How about the Crab Cooker?"

"Sounds perfect."

I had second thoughts as I directed him to Pacific Coast Highway and over the Newport Boulevard Bridge toward the peninsula. This was Leo's stomping grounds. Maybe I shouldn't be bringing a date over here. Still, it was pretty safe. He'd be in the middle of his baseball game right now. A bit of guilt made my stomach churn as I remembered the look on his face the day before, pleading for me to come.

Henry continued to drive along, looking comfortable enough behind the wheel. "So, Dove, tell me something. Why don't you have a boyfriend?"

I spun to meet his question. Could he read my mind? "Well, funny you should ask..." I stopped myself and glanced out the window into the dark night. That was a stupid thing to say. There was nothing funny about it. "I just broke up with someone, actually."

"Ah. The chap you were with at the fair?"

All I could do was nod as I looked out the window, staring at the lights that blurred past as we sped along. It was more than weird to discuss Leo with another guy.

Henry smoothly changed the conversation to relationships in general as the bright red restaurant came into view, its neon sign glowing above its green-striped awning.

Inside, we sat down across from each other at a small table, still engaged in a discussion that had somehow now moved to my plans for the future.

"San Francisco sounds lovely," Henry said, talking over the noise of the restaurant. He made a menacing face as he pointed to a shark hanging from the ceiling above us, its mouth propped open to show a large circle of sharp teeth.

I laughed. "I got accepted to schools in Savannah, Chicago and Paris, too. I'm wondering now if I should change my mind."

"Further away from home has its advantages. It all depends upon the person," he said, dipping his head sideways. "Only you can decide what's best, really."

Eating off paper plates and cracking crab legs together gave our dinner a casual, relaxed tone, and somehow Henry smoothly steered the conversation right back around to my breakup with Leo. This time I was ready to talk.

"I got too caught up in my emotions, I think. Now I just need to use my head, you know, be more logical about everything," I said, shrugging. Henry gave me a sideways glance but didn't say anything. I shot him a frown. "Do you have a thought on that?"

He took a bite of crab with his plastic fork and slowly chewed it. "Sounds to me like you're in danger of shutting down your heart. To be an artist means you have to allow yourself to feel."

My head swooned. This guy was talking about artistry and feelings, and his haughty British accent just made him sound even more brilliant.

"Your intuition, your soul, are what feed your creativity. You can choose not to be with him and still leave your heart open." He pushed his plate away and leaned back in his chair, his face full of intensity.

I studied his relaxed expression. How did he know so much? He was pretty mature and wise for twenty-two. Was it a European thing?

"What do you think of Audrey Hepburn?" I blurted. My sudden question made his eyebrows jump.

"Audrey Hepburn?" His British way of pronouncing her name made me smile as he continued, "Well, I suppose I think what most everyone thinks—she's fantastic. An icon in every way."

My eyes narrowed in interest, and I nodded at him.

He leaned forward into the table, reading the intrigue on my face. "Audrey," he said, his accent almost a whisper. "Now there's someone who kept her heart open at every turn."

I blinked at him for a long moment, letting his words soak in.

"So." He straightened in his chair, changing his tone from serious to fun again. "What's for dessert?"

I didn't hesitate. "You have to try a Balboa Bar if you really want to taste Newport Beach. And we'll go across on the ferry to get one."

HENRY JOKED ABOUT ACCIDENTALLY bumping the cars in front of us into the bay as he carefully steered onto the ferry, easing to a stop behind the first two cars. As the ferry lurched forward to make the short trip across the bay, he slipped one arm around me without a word and leaned me onto his shoulder.

I felt the warmth of his breath against my ear as he bent his head to mine. "This is fun," he whispered.

My pulse quickened. I hadn't even thought of the prospect of kissing him yet, but here and now was the ideal moment for a kiss—if that's what he had in mind. I stole a quick glance at his face, but he simply stared contentedly at the lights sparkling across the dark water of the bay. False alarm. I exhaled slowly. But was I relieved or disappointed? I relaxed my head against his shoulder and watched alongside him in silence as the ferry finished its trip, slowly pulling into the Balboa Island landing.

We parked on Marine Avenue, and I guided Henry along the sidewalk to the Sugar 'n' Spice ice cream shop. Together, we leaned into the walk-up window beneath the giant frozen banana sign and watched while the girl dipped a vanilla ice cream bar into melted chocolate and then covered it in nuts and candy sprinkles.

I held it out to Henry. "This is a Balboa Bar," I said with fake seriousness. "You haven't lived until you've tried one."

Henry crunched into it, insisting I share it with him as he pulled me beside him onto the green wooden bench. I played along, keeping up with him by taking one bite for each of his.

A large flake of hardened chocolate fell from the side of the ice cream, and he grabbed for it. "That's mine!" he said, laughing.

I whisked it out of his fingers, trying to hold it out of reach. "Wow! What happened to sharing?"

His jaw dropped. "You already ate most of the chocolate!" He pointed at me and then at the chocolate in my hand. "That's my piece!"

Another chocolate lover. There seemed to be nothing wrong with this guy. Not one chink in the armor. He locked eyes with mine, and his grin faded just slightly as I studied his face. I finally rolled my eyes and surrendered with a sigh, holding the piece of chocolate out toward him.

Chapter 28

"I'VE SPOILED YOUR EVENING, HAVEN'T I?"
-SABRINA FAIRCHILD

Sabrina

Henry turned the car onto my street. It was late and the lane echoed with emptiness. So different from the daytime, when kids ran from house to house and threw dirt clods in the empty lot. I remembered being one of them, riding down the street on my bike with the basket attached. It didn't feel like very long ago. Leaning forward, I pointed to the right toward my gray-and-white house.

Then I saw it, over on the left.

Oh, no. Oh, crap. Leo's blue Bronco.

My chest tightened as Henry's car rolled to a stop. "Uh oh," I said, at a loss for any other words.

"What is it?" Henry asked.

I stared across the street and tried to steady my breath at the sight of Leo sitting in the passenger seat, his face hard and angry. Clive was sitting in the driver's seat, looking out of place and uncomfortable.

"Um, Henry, this is extremely awkward..." As I spoke

I didn't move my eyes from Leo. "I'm so sorry, but..."

Henry looked in the direction of my gaze. "Ah—the ex-boyfriend?" His voice stayed quiet, steady.

I nodded, my eyes still glued to Leo's. Damn it. How dare he sit out there like a stalker.

A slow heat crept up, burning my cheeks. Why did it feel like I'd just been caught? I hadn't done anything wrong. His dark eyes bored into mine. What next? My stomach churned. Would he come at Henry and force him to fight, like some kind of old-fashioned duel?

The horrific thought made me turn to open the car door. Henry reached out, putting his hand on my arm. "Play it calmly," he said.

"Get your hands off her!" Leo sprang from his seat onto the opposite sidewalk and strode forward. Henry got out of the car, and I stepped onto the sidewalk in front of the lawn. Leo walked across the street, heading straight toward Henry.

"Oh, are you on a date?" he taunted.

Is he drunk? If his glossed-over eyes didn't prove it, his belligerence did. *Please don't swing at him, Leo,* I begged from inside my head.

"Leo, stop it!" I shouted, quickly walking between the two guys, trying to make myself into a human barrier. Henry stood his ground, square-shouldered and quiet. Leo's eyes were wild with anger as he searched my face, and I realized there would be no reasoning with him in his drunk and livid state. I stood frozen for a moment, unsure what to do.

"Please go, Leo," I said, trying with all my might to sound calm and collected. I looked past his shoulder at Clive, still sitting in the driver's seat. He just shrugged at me.

"I thought you didn't want to date anyone. What

happened to *that*?" I could smell the alcohol on his breath as he moved even closer. "You needed time to be alone, *remember*?" His eyes pierced into mine, I had never seen him this angry. My mind reeled. *How can this be happening?* Seconds ticked by in slow motion.

Still in the forefront of my mind was the horrible thought of Henry being forced into a fight. I barely knew him. I could just picture him unable to perform the next day because of a black eye or a knocked-out tooth, and it would be all my fault. I had to be firm. Leo needed to go before things got out of hand.

"Leave *now*, Leo," I demanded, my eyes locking with his.

His expression twisted with anger as he leaned his face into mine. "I despise you—*you lying, selfish bitch*."

Stunned, I attempted to blink away my surprise. In what seemed like a split second, I stepped forward, lifted my arm and slapped him across the face with all of my strength. My hand stung as I took a step back, halfway disbelieving what I had just done. Leo stood still, his eyes never moving from mine. My head spun with the chaos of the moment, but I planted my feet, willing myself to be steady.

After what seemed like an eternal pause, Leo broke his gaze and glanced at the sky, rubbing the back of his head. His hand lingered to grab his neck. My favorite little habit of his. How different and terrible it was to watch it now.

Without another word he turned, walking away from me and across the street without the smallest glance in Henry's direction. The Bronco started, its wheels crushing against the asphalt as Clive drove them away.

I turned to Henry, apologizing with my eyes.

He offered a kind smile. "Well, Dove." His crisp accent was still cheerful. "It seems you have a bit of Shakespearean drama of your very own," he said, pulling me to his chest and wrapping his arms around me.

I couldn't help thinking how mature and man-like he seemed as I shut my eyes, my head still swimming. How could Leo do it? I hated him and still loved him at the same time. I wasn't sure if I would ever be able to stop loving him. And all of a sudden, here was Henry—sexy, smart, and spouting Shakespeare. The labyrinth of thoughts just twisted into a bigger and even more confusing maze in my mind.

After holding me in silence for what seemed like a full minute, Henry walked me up the front steps, reassuring me in his agreeable way. I stepped inside and closed the front door, leaning back against it for a moment with my eyes closed. What was I doing? This wasn't a 1950's old Hollywood film. *Girls can't just go around slapping guys across the face anymore.* No matter how much they deserved it.

Chapter 29

Eucalyptus leaves crunched beneath our flip-flops as Jessie and I hiked down the dirt footpath and through the tunnel with our beach bags slung over our shoulders. Waves crashed along the empty shore, with only a couple of young kids splashing in the surf. Jessie's suggestion of Crystal Cove was the perfect idea for the antisocial mood I had found myself in lately. The tucked-away beach was more low-key in the off-season, and since it was down the coast toward Laguna, it lessened the possibility of running into anyone we knew... especially Leo.

He didn't show up to English class on Friday, and I was beyond relieved not to have to face him after the night before. As jerk-like as he had behaved, I wished I had not stooped so low as to slap him. In true gentlemanlike fashion, Henry had called Friday morning and left a polite, had-a-nice-time message on my voicemail, but I couldn't bring myself to call him back with the embarrassment of the night's end still so fresh in my memory.

Jessie laid her towel on the sand, peeled off her shorts and T-shirt, and ran into the water. I followed her lead, but lagged behind a bit, stopping when the water reached my knees. I watched as her red bikini disappeared under a wave.

Her head poked out of the water. "Chicken!" she shouted.

I stood my ground, allowing the whitewater to rush against me. "You know I don't like the waves! The undertow freaks me out!"

"C'mon, there's no riptide! Look at the flag." She pointed to the lifeguard stand where a small green flag flapped in the breeze. "Green!"

I ran back to our pile on the sand and grabbed Jessie's swim fins out of her bag. Hopping through the wet sand, I pulled the fins onto my feet, then splashed through the whitewash and ducked under the first breaker.

After half an hour in the water, I flopped onto my towel next to Jessie, my skin tingling from the saltwater, and laid my head sideways against the sand to look out at the ocean. For a moment I paused, breathing it all in, taking in the entire view. My mind flashed to Audrey admiring the streets of Paris from her apartment window, and Sabrina's words echoed in my head. She'd talked about being herself in the world and learning how to truly live life, instead of just watching from the sidelines.

I closed my eyes against the sun. That's what I wanted. It's what I had always wanted. But I'd been standing aside and watching lately. When had I last picked up a paintbrush? I hadn't painted or drawn anything for fun in months.

"You hungry?" I sat upright, looking up the cliff toward Ruby's Shake Shack. "I want a snack," I said, digging through my bag for my drawing pad. "And I want to sketch the beach from up there."

WITH A SHAKE IN one hand, I balanced the pad of paper on my knees and penciled the outline of the ocean below. Jessie sat on the bench next to me, gnawing on a hot dog, when my phone rang out from my shorts pocket.

I fumbled for it, hesitating for a moment at the name glaring at me, and then answered. "Hi, Henry."

"Hello again, Dove."

"Henry..." The memory of the whole fiasco in the street popped up. "Um..." It was weird to have shared such a personal moment with a guy I barely knew. I rubbed my forehead, wondering if I should say anything more about it.

"How are you? I'd love to see you again," he said without missing a beat. "Shall we have another go? Would Thursday work?"

Apparently, the whole Leo thing hadn't chased him away at all. My stomach did a flip, not letting me deny the fact that I did want to see him again. "I can't. I've got a chemistry test on Friday. I have to study. I'm free on the weekend, but you're probably working, right?"

"Yes—and Sunday's our last day. We leave Monday for New York." He paused, and I reconsidered the idea of studying. Maybe I could just wing it.

"I've got it," he said. "Come to the theater Sunday

afternoon. I'll show you around before the matinee. You can hang around backstage with me."

"Backstage?" A breeze blew across the cliff top, making my skin tingle. Or was it the thought of a behind-the-scenes tour with Henry that had done it? Regardless, another whole week dealing with the hassle of avoiding Leo might not be so hard to take with something fun and interesting to look forward to. "Yes." I smiled. "Perfect."

HENRY RAN DOWN THE steps of the theater to greet me, his navy crewneck T-shirt contrasting perfectly against his wavy, blond hair. A sudden rush of heat warmed my face when he flashed a playful look at me before guiding me through the back entrance. Inside the backstage area, workers and stagehands were running here and there, carting items around. A few management people stood around talking, preoccupied with one thing or another.

"We have two hours until the start of the show. I'll need to get dressed in a bit," he informed me as he led me along.

"Oh goody, I get to see you in that rockin' outfit again," I teased.

"I'll have you know, it was all the rage in the 1500s," he said, faking seriousness as we continued to weave our way through old set decorations and stacks of props. He introduced me to a few people we passed while pointing out different behind-the-scenes things of interest.

"Over here," he said, guiding me over to a doorway. He looked at me pointedly, raising one eyebrow as he turned the door handle. "The Audrey Hepburn in you is going to love this."

My breath caught when we stepped into a room

overflowing with frilled Renaissance-style dresses. It was as much fabric eye candy as I'd ever seen in one place. The rich colors and textures swept me right into the magic of the sixteenth century, and I imagined myself swishing around in all of the rich fabric, feeling regal and important. Yes, lucky Audrey. This was pure fashion bliss. There was no doubt she must have relished all the dresses and costume rooms she encountered. I reached out to touch the silky edge of a blue dress hanging next to me, secretly wishing I could throw it on over my jeans.

"Knew you'd love it." Henry looked pleased with himself as he ushered me out of the costume room and toward a back entrance to the stage. He pulled on a small door, holding it open for me, and I recognized the front of it. It was the carved wooden door that had opened and closed in the center of the stage so many times during the performance. "After you." His arm extended out toward the empty stage.

I walked ahead of him, my footsteps echoing as I made my way to the middle, turning around three hundred and sixty degrees to take it all in. The gilded stage glowed almost mysteriously in its silence. Thousands of empty seats stared back at me, and I couldn't help but revel in the grand scope of the huge place.

Henry perched himself on a raised platform to the right, and I remembered when he had sat in the exact same spot during the performance, spilling out line after line of Shakespeare.

"That's where you gave one of your speeches," I said.

He only nodded.

"It blew me away. I could barely follow the words. They were so expressive and… complicated…" I turned, shaking my head at him. "How can you possibly remember all of that?"

His mouth twitched downward in thought as he hopped down and walked toward me. "I don't know. It's just natural to me. That's like me asking how you paint so beautifully." He stopped in front of me, not taking his eyes from my face.

His closeness took me by surprise. I let out a scoff, attempting an air of casualness. "You've never even seen my paintings."

He moved in. "But I want to." His eyes flicked over my face and his fingers wrapped around me, pressing into my waist as his lips slowly closed in on mine.

His kiss became deeper as the seconds ticked by. I leaned into him, completely drawn in by the softness of his skin, the way he moved his mouth against mine.

My thoughts began to wander. Suddenly, it felt strange to be touched by another guy. Despite my best efforts, Leo's face had emerged into my mind before the kiss had finished.

Henry pulled me to him playfully. "You're a great kisser."

A tiny bit of guilt crept up, and I tried to smile it away. It was Leo who had taught me how to kiss, really. His confidence, his wild way with life, his intensity... all of that translated to his kisses. I stared out at the sea of red velvet seats. Time to change the subject. "So, this is what it feels like to be up here."

Henry let go of me and stepped down the stage. "Quite nice, isn't it?" he asked, opening his arms out to the emptiness.

I wasn't so sure. I gazed out, imagining three thousand pairs of eyes fixed only on me. Quite nice vacant. Yes. But, filled with people? Not so much. "It doesn't scare you at all?"

"On the contrary, I feed off the excitement of it," he

said, his eyebrows shooting up as he pulled me toward the little doorway again.

Backstage, even more people buzzed around behind the scenery now. A group of actresses in costume said hi to Henry when we passed, nodding as he introduced me. Then he stopped me in front of a wooden chair.

"Right," he said in his British way. "I need to get into costume." I smiled as he continued, "You sit here, and when I come back I'll dare you to kiss a man wearing tights."

"Can't wait." I gave him my best bring-it-on look. "I love dares."

When he returned in full costume, I couldn't help marveling at the overall effect of it. His fitted, old-world jacket accentuated every muscle in his body, his jaw framed by the white collar underneath. A worn, leather satchel was slung across his chest.

He beamed at the look on my face. "I knew you'd like it—after all, you couldn't take your eyes off me the other night." He came to a standstill in front of me, pulling me to my feet. The comment caught me off-guard, giving me no chance to hide. His eyes bolted themselves to mine as my cheeks began to tingle with heat.

He had no mercy. "Is that a blush I see?" He bent closer, drawing me to him with a playful smile. "Methinks the lovely Juliet has fallen for her Romeo."

My stomach tightly twisted as the words fell out of his mouth. I looked at the floor and let out a polite laugh, while all of a sudden feeling like a two-timing, heartless witch. The fact that I had officially broken up with Leo didn't seem to matter to my heart—or my head. Both wouldn't stop reminding me of him.

Chapter 30

"Let's walk together quietly, and I'll try and help you understand."
-Holly Golightly

Breakfast at Tiffany's

As I made my way through the crowded school hallway, I let my eyes pause on details I'd never bothered to give much attention—the thick windows of the classroom doors sandwiched between rows of gray, dented lockers—I tried to burn the images into my memory. Only three days to go. All around me, people rushed along through the chaos of finals week. I couldn't help thinking how different the end of the year turned out to be, compared to its beginning—and compared to what I imagined it would be like with Leo. It was a good thing Henry's troupe had traveled on. He really was a charming guy with all of his Shakespeare smarts, but his presence seemed to only confuse me even more.

Choosing a school had been somewhat straightforward when Leo was in the picture. But lately, the wheels turning in my head had begun to backpedal. Was it too late to change my mind? The idea of going to

Chicago actually didn't seem half bad now. And what about Paris? How could I have passed up studying in Europe just like that?

I tensed at the sight of Piper up ahead, walking toward me. She waved before I had a chance to look away. "Hi," she said, coming to a stop in front of me.

"Hi." I was the one not smiling this time. *Rumor starter*. How dare she act like nothing had happened.

She glanced away and bit her lip. "I... I just want you to know something." She shifted her weight as her eyes met mine again.

"Okay," I said. Questions began to pop up and race each other in my head.

"I never told anyone that I saw you guys in Santa Barbara."

Wait... what? My eyes scoured her face for a hint of dishonesty, a shred of a lie. But she just stood there, the picture of blinking sincerity, her eyes hesitant, waiting for my response.

"Then who did?" I blurted, my mind filing back through the possibilities.

She shook her head. "I really don't know."

"Okay." I nodded at the floor. "Thanks for telling me." What else was there to say? Jessie must have been right, then. One way or another, it had been leaked through the grapevine, but it really didn't matter anymore. The image of Piper standing on the beach in Santa Barbara with her sketchpad in hand flashed in my mind, and a little bit of that old respect for her crept back in. *She'd* never lost focus on her art. And she hadn't told my secret after all.

"I heard you're going to SFAI next year," she said, adjusting the bag on her shoulder. "It turns out I'm going there, too."

Wow. Being on friendly terms again was one thing, but the same college? That was a little more than I was prepared for. "Really?" I asked, trying to sound cheerful about it.

She motioned down the hallway with her head, and we began to walk together. "So, I thought, you know, maybe we could get together and compare notes on classes and stuff."

My mind wandered devilishly. *That's not all we could compare notes on.* A hot jealousy popped up at the thought of Leo kissing her... touching her... my thoughts dared to wander even further. How far had the two of them actually gone? "Um, yeah, we could do that. Compare notes, I mean."

The reality of going to the same school as Piper began to sink in. Actually, knowing someone might be a good thing, and the truth was that Piper could be pretty nice when she wasn't busy defending her territory. Still, the annoying, competitive thing probably wasn't going to just disappear all of a sudden. The way it hovered over the two of us seemed to perpetually prevent any chance of just having a normal friendship.

We rounded the corner outside toward the winding path to the science building. Looking up ahead, my heart jumped in my chest.

Leo.

We had succeeded in avoiding each other since the whole front yard incident. But now he was walking down the pathway in our direction, staring at the ground with his backpack slung over one shoulder. With grass on both sides, the cement walkway was not wide enough for more than two people. I fell silent. Piper stopped talking, too, and I stopped myself from even glancing in her direction.

Now less than ten feet away, Leo finally looked up. Piper and I kept walking straight ahead, side by side, without slowing our pace. Leo stepped sideways onto the grass, passing us without a word. My instinct to ignore him kicked in as usual, but this time I couldn't listen to my own advice. I allowed my eyes to meet his.

Sadness was all I saw this time. The anger must have left along with the Bacardi or the beer, or whatever it was that he'd had that night. I broke my gaze first, pulling my eyes from his, and continued on in perfect lockstep, shoulder to shoulder with Piper.

Chapter 31

"'If I were dead and buried and I heard your voice beneath the sod, my heart of dust would still rejoice.' Do you know that poem?"
-Princess Ann

Roman Holiday

I swung open my closet door and stared at the green dress hanging in front of me. Choosing it had been easy. It was the only one I liked in the entire boutique, and I'd quickly decided on it, having not been in the mood to scour all of Newport Beach for a graduation dress.

Pulling it over my head, I turned to see my reflection in the mirror. The silky fabric shined in its deep shade of emerald, and the boat neckline and sleeveless, fitted bodice accentuated all the right places. Not too shabby. *Sabrina*-esque. Audrey would definitely approve.

I stared at myself, unable to ignore the emptiness in my eyes. Two months without Leo and still I had to admit that my heart wanted him. Had I been wrong not to forgive him? Was I being too stubborn? Maybe a love like ours shouldn't be ignored or given up on. Maybe it deserved another chance. Should his moment of weakness determine our lives? And would I ever feel as much for another guy? No answers came. Only more questions. Questions I had no doubt my mom would have tried to help answer. If only she were still here.

I grabbed my navy blue cap and gown and flicked off the light, slowing for a moment in the doorway to slide my hand against Audrey's shiny poster.

"**TONIGHT IS GONNA BE** the best ever!" Jessie shouted to no one in particular as we walked in a group toward the football field. She broke into a run and lifted her arms, the sleeves of her graduation gown flapping in the air. "A grad night harbor cruise!! Woohooo!"

The yacht thing was the big buzz. Everyone would spend the entire night until dawn on the boat together. The thought of being in the middle of all that happiness with Leo just sitting in the corner depressed as ever sucked all the fun out of it for me. But then again, he probably wouldn't even show up to it.

In the stadium, the stands were filled with family and friends waiting for the ceremony to begin. Chairs had been laid out in rows on the green turf for the graduates, and everyone filed in to take their seats in alphabetical order the way we had practiced.

Jessie turned to me before she headed for her chair. "See you in a few. Don't trip or anything," she said, shooting me a huge grin as I squeezed sideways through my row of chairs. Too bad Walsh was nowhere near Courtland alphabetically... an annoying little detail ever since the first grade.

The ceremony began with inspirational speeches

213

filling the open field, making my thoughts wander right to my mom again. If only she were in the audience to see me graduate—how different this day would have been. No doubt, how different the year would have been if she'd been here to see me through it. As it was, on my own I'd managed to make a pretty big mess of it.

A light breeze blew across the grass, tossing my hat's tassel like a silent chime against my face as the ritualistic doling out of diplomas began and the names of each graduate started to echo out one by one. "Dove Courtland," finally rang from the loud speakers. I stood and walked down the long aisle, feeling the weight of Leo's eyes upon me the entire time as the principal shook my hand and handed me the diploma. More names boomed from the speaker system. As soon as I took my seat, his name sounded. I watched him take his diploma and then looked away as he walked back down the aisle and sat down just two rows away.

At the end of the ceremony, everyone stood and cheered as hundreds of navy blue caps flew into the air and the guests spilled onto the football field to join the graduates. My family surrounded me, hugging and congratulating me while the crowd milled around us.

Aunt Gail grabbed me. "You've got so much ahead of you," she said, squeezing me tightly.

I found a smile while wondering just what, in fact, was ahead of me. The whole idea of your-future-lies-before-you didn't really feel like it was all it was cracked up to be. There was no guarantee about what paths to choose. So far, this whole entire future thing had been as confusing as ever.

Off to the left, a roar of voices lifted above the already noisy crowd and carried over toward me. Leo was circled by a swarm of cheering, shouting people.

Isaiah slapped him on the back as Clive and a bunch of other guys surrounded him. His mom stood a few feet away, smiling in a flowing dress. His dad was next to him, beaming and babbling all at once.

"Giants! Fifth-round draft pick! Just got the news!" His dad called out to the principal as she approached the loud group.

That's right. MLB Draft Day. Today, June ninth. And Leo had got his wish… the San Francisco Giants. He looked genuinely happy for the first time in months. Tears welled. I should have been over there, too, reveling in the good news with him. This was supposed to have been our moment to celebrate and laugh together.

I drew in a slow breath, restraining myself in the joy of the moment from running over to him and throwing my arms around his neck. But still, I told myself, congratulating him might be the right thing to do. The kind, mature thing. I glimpsed in the direction of my dad. He and Patty were deep in conversation with a bunch of other parents. He probably wouldn't notice. But if he did, then so be it. Maybe it was time to tell him everything anyway.

I let the moment guide me, allowing myself to walk toward Leo. Moving into the group of people surrounding him, I reached out and laid my hand on his arm.

When he turned toward me, his eyes widened. "Dove." He looked surprised and pleased, and he didn't attempt to hide either one.

"I just wanted to say congratulations," I said. Tears welled. "I'm really happy for you."

He reached out and grabbed my elbows, then let go as though he had forgotten everything for an instant, all of a sudden realizing the reality of the distance now between us. He flashed a look at the ground and then to me. "Thank you, Dove. It means a lot."

I tilted my head and then shifted my weight, searching for a comfortable position. "Looks like your dad is pretty happy with the Giants after all."

He raised his eyebrows and let out a breath, nodding in his dad's direction. "Yeah."

I stared at him, my mind still trying to grasp the fact that we were no longer together, still trying to grasp what he did, and arguing with myself over the meaning of it all. The chaos and the crowd continued to swirl around both of us as we stood there, our eyes locked on each other.

He swallowed. "I miss you."

I looked away, out toward the mass of people swarming the green turf. A few tears escaped onto my cheeks, and I brushed them away as I turned back to him, nodding. "I miss you, too."

"Leo! I want you to meet someone!" his dad's voice boomed from behind us.

"Okay, be right there," he called over his shoulder. He turned back to me, studying my face one more time. "Will you be there tonight? At grad night?" He was searching for a shred of hope. Something inside of me wanted to help him find it.

"Mmhmm." I gave a quick nod.

"Okay." He looked glad about it and then slowed himself down. "Maybe—maybe I'll see you there," he said, shooting me a half smile as he reluctantly turned away.

I steered myself in the direction of my family. Patty and my dad were still talking away. Griffin looked as bored as ever, kicking at a tall tuft of grass with the toe of his shoe.

"Hey Griff." I realized I hadn't even thought of the fact that I was really going to miss him when I went away. "Want me to spin you?"

"Okay!" His face brightened.

I grabbed him, pulling him backward to an open space on the field, away from the crowd. Holding him tight, I swung him around, spinning him faster and faster until the pressure was too much. He burst out laughing as I finally spun to a stop, tossing him onto the grass. I dropped beside him to catch my breath, then closed my eyes and waited for my dizzy head to right itself.

Chapter 32

"I'VE HEARD OF A WONDERFUL PLACE FOR DANCING
ON A BOAT."
-PRINCESS ANN

Roman Holiday

We sat in silence as Jessie's Jeep bumped along on its way to the peninsula marina.

"I cannot believe we graduated. It's so surreal," Jessie said, steering into the large parking lot beside the commercial boat docks.

"It's pretty amazing," I agreed, half listening.

"You okay?"

I stared into nothingness. "Think I should forgive him?"

"No." Jessie's tone turned serious as she pulled the Jeep into an open spot. "But that's not for me to say."

The huge harbor cruise yacht sat waiting in its slip, its lights twinkling in the dusk. Several kids were making their way toward the gangplank, but the boat looked like it was already crawling with people.

"Are we late?" Jessie frowned. "Everyone's already here."

"It's seven forty-five—the boat leaves at eight," I answered, wondering if Leo had arrived yet. "Did you talk to Isaiah? Or Clive and Kai?"

"They aren't coming," Jessie said, hopping out. "They're going to take Clive's Boston Whaler out and ride alongside the boat all night. A few people are doing that, actually."

"Oh." I tried my best not to sound disappointed. "Leo might be with them."

Jessie shot me a give-me-a-break look as we walked down the creaky planks of the dock. "Uh, I don't think so, Dove. This is his big day, with the baseball draft and everything? Besides, he knows he'll be near you the whole night if he's on the yacht."

"What about you?" I eyed her sideways, but she didn't respond. "What about Isaiah?"

She shook her head and pulled the band from her ponytail, tossing her long hair behind her. "Kai invited me, but Isaiah never said a word about it, so there's no way I was going to do it. Not that it matters—I want to ride on the yacht anyway." She hooked her arm into mine, pulling me along. "And I want to be with my Dovey."

We joined the line at the security checkpoint and then looked up together at the glossy bow of the massive boat.

"Wow," Jessie said as we stepped aboard. "This doesn't disappoint." She weaved her way through the crowd and then headed toward the stairwell to the upper decks. I followed close behind, scanning for any sign of Leo.

We rounded the stairwell to the second tier and ended up in the middle of a crowded, shiny black dance floor. The booming beat of the bass blasted from the speakers.

At the far end next to a glass window, Leo was sitting in the middle of a group of guys. They laughed together in what looked like more celebrating over the draft. Midsentence, he caught a glimpse of me. Right away he nodded his head at the guy next to him and stood up, heading straight toward me.

"Hi." He inspected me.

"Hi." I shifted my weight.

He turned to Jessie. "Hey, Jess."

Jessie gave him a civil wave.

"So..." Leo paused, rubbing his neck. "Are you guys hungry... thirsty? There's tons of food upstairs."

I looked at Jessie and then back to Leo. "Um, sure. Something to drink sounds good."

The three of us climbed the last flight of stairs to the upper deck, reaching the top just as the horn blared and the huge cruiser headed out of its slip for the night. A bunch of kids cheered as the boat began to cut through the water.

For the next hour, Leo didn't move more than two feet from my side, and I secretly honed in on the details of his every movement. Wrapped up in a baseball discussion, he joked around with the guys standing near him. Next to me, a girl from my chemistry class was trying to make conversation.

"So, yeah... political science, because I want to go to law school," she said.

"Jessie's pre-law, too," I said, doing all I could in my distracted state to sound interested. "She's going to Boston College. You guys should talk more about that."

Beside me, Leo's voice rose and fell in conversation. One ear listened to him and the other to the girl I barely knew who was now going on about the coed dorms at

NYU.

A tingling sensation crawled up my arm as I felt the gentle touch of Leo's fingertips against my hand. I glanced at him sideways. He continued his discussion as though nothing was happening, while weaving his fingers into mine. I kept responding to the girl's chitchat, unable to get my mind off the warm pressure of Leo's hand against mine. He carried on with his casual conversation for the next five minutes without letting go, and I gripped his hand in return.

With a quick squeeze, he turned to me. "Want something to eat now?"

"Yes." I was hungrier than I had been in months.

"You go ahead," the girl said. "My stomach feels a little queasy. Maybe I'm seasick or something."

"Oh no—feel better," I said as she walked away. Seasick? Was it even possible to get seasick on the bay?

Leo pulled me over toward some cushioned seats, away from the crowd. His eyes studied my every move, but he said nothing.

"I thought we were getting something to eat," I said, sliding onto the bench seat.

He squeezed in next to me. "That was just an excuse. I wanted to be alone with you."

I lowered my eyes. It was happening. This was what I wanted, right? What I secretly hoped for? But what if I was completely wrong about it all?

"I don't know if this is a good idea, Leo." I shook my head, blinking at him.

"No..." He reached out for my hand, stopping me. "Please just listen, Dove. I could never hurt you again. Never. You're everything to me. We can't just walk away from what we have together. And with the Giants drafting me, you have to admit, it all seems meant to be."

221

He bent toward me, grabbing my head with both hands and moving his lips to within an inch of mine. "We," he moved his gaze from my eyes to my lips, "are meant to be." He closed in, determined to kiss me, determined to show me with his mouth what he felt in his heart, and I let him.

He moved his lips to my neck. "I missed you so much, Birdy." He leaned back and squinted as his eyes roamed my face, taking me in. "This is my best day."

I grabbed onto him, reveling in the feeling of being near him again. Together. Connected. The way it should be. My world was finally righting itself.

But my thoughts still whirled in circles. What was I doing? Surely I couldn't just take him back after everything that had happened, could I? But then again, what could be wrong with giving someone a second chance? No, not just someone. Leo. My Leo. Leo—who I loved and adored and missed with every fiber of myself. I pulled him to me as though close still wasn't close enough and laid my head against the collar of his shirt, breathing in his scent. "I missed you, Leo. But I'm just not sure... I don't know..."

His sturdy arms squeezed me, and he bent his head toward mine, his hair falling into my face, softly brushing my cheek. "Don't decide now... just think about it," he whispered.

I rolled my head against his shoulder to look out at the bay. A handful of boats were gliding along beside the yacht. "It's Clive and Kai!" I pointed.

Leo stood and leaned over the high railing. "Hey, guys!"

Down below, Clive looked up from the bow of his Boston Whaler, waving a can of beer back and forth. "You're missing out!"

222

Leo shouted back at Clive, and I spotted Greta sitting beside Nate in an electric Duffy farther out, its overhead canvas awning flapping in the breeze. It was the perfect little boat for a quiet harbor cruise. I smiled at the two of them looking so cozy together.

Leo led me down the stairs, and we made our way hand in hand across the dance floor to a table by the window. Every pair of eyes in the room seemed to turn and examine us, but I breathed deeply and ignored the invisible spotlight, instead focusing on Leo's eyes—Leo's hair—Leo's laughter. All the things I had missed for the past two months. I reached out and gently placed my hand on his arm, relishing the feeling of his muscles beneath the softness of his shirt. Our conversation slowed, and his face faded into a heavy happiness as he leaned in to kiss me again. I had no idea how many people might still be watching us, and I didn't care anymore. I was tired of thinking, tired of analyzing, tired of figuring out the right thing to do. In the end, it all boiled down to the fact that I wanted Leo, and Leo wanted me.

"Leooooo!" one of his baseball buddies howled out as he crossed the room toward us. I seized the moment to slip away with a quick little wave, leaving Leo to more baseball talk so I could set off to the lower deck to find the bathrooms.

The usual crowd of girls around the restroom was nowhere to be seen, and the narrow hallway was empty until I stepped back out into it, almost bumping into Piper, who stood waiting in the narrow corridor.

For a brief moment, we stood in silence with only the drone of the engine and the muffled beat of the music to fill the void.

"I see you and Leo are back together again," she said.

Her tone was... what? Definitely not angry. Matter-of-fact? No. What was it then?

My eyes shot sideways and then back to her. The right words to say to her wouldn't materialize. I tried to assess her attitude again. She looked... *sympathetic.*

She studied me with a slow, careful sweep of her eyes. "I guess that means you haven't heard about Clarissa."

My heartbeat picked up. "What about Clarissa?"

Piper bit her lips together, took a deep breath, and looked straight into my eyes. "She's pregnant."

The words hit me like a punch. My stomach tightened, and my whole body froze as my mind reeled.

The door next to us clicked as someone emerged from the other bathroom. We both turned to see Jude step out, her eyes narrow with seriousness. "It's true. Clarissa's telling everyone that her dad's making her keep it, and that he wants Leo to take responsibility."

I looked from Jude to Piper and back again. Nausea swirled in my gut. Could it be true? I tried to stop my spinning thoughts. What about considering the source? After all, these were basically my enemies, standing in front of me, informing me of the most terrible news ever.

"Dove!" Jessie bounded alongside me, frowning. "We have to talk." At the look on my face and the serious stares of Piper and Jude, Jessie put it together. "Oh, no. They told you, didn't they? I just heard. I was coming to find you."

Now there would be no denying it. The sick feeling surged all through me, with thoughts of my future with Leo smashed to pieces. How could this be? Ten minutes ago, he had declared his love and honesty. I blinked at the floor. "I have to get off."

"The boat?" Piper frowned.

"Yes. I need to get off. I don't want to see him."

"That's impossible," Jude chimed in. I braced for one of her rude remarks as she continued. "The whole purpose of Grad Night is to keep us together in one place with no chance of drinking and driving. I think you're pretty much stuck here for the night." She actually sounded genuine about it. Great. Even the likes of Jude pitied me.

"She's right," Jessie said. "They won't let you off until the morning."

"Maybe you could tell them you're sick or something," Piper offered.

Jessie shook her head. "There's no way. A girl upstairs just puked over the side, and they wouldn't let her leave." She grabbed my arm. "C'mon. Let's get you some fresh air. You look like you just might puke, too."

We headed outside as the yacht cruised along through the harbor, the music from the upper decks blaring into the sky. Only a few people dotted the lower deck. Jessie ushered me over to the railing and stood beside me in silence as my heart pounded harder and harder at the nightmare just revealed to me. I leaned forward into the breeze and closed my eyes, waiting for the sobs to come, but the shock had only brought with it an eerie quiet this time. "I can't believe it. We were almost back together tonight. It was all going to be amazing again."

Out on the water, Nate's electric Duffy chugged along through the darkness, making slow circles around the yacht. Greta was still wedged beside him, looking content as ever as they talked under the striped awning.

It came to me. The perfect idea. I leaned over the railing a bit further. "Greta!" I shouted. "Can I get a ride?"

Jessie spun toward me. "Really?"

"What? Are you serious?" Greta shouted.

"Yes! Can you get close enough for me to hop on?" My voice traveled across the water, and I hoped no one would catch on, especially Leo. Time was ticking. He'd probably come to look for me any minute now.

Greta said something to Nate, and a few seconds later the little Duffy headed straight toward the yacht.

Suddenly, the cruiser's horn blared. The huge speakers above and around us crackled and then boomed with a loud voice. "*ATTENTION. ALL VESSELS FOLLOWING OR CIRCLING THIS YACHT MUST DISPERSE IMMEDIATELY. THE HARBOR PATROL HAS BEEN NOTIFIED.*"

Now only fifty feet away, Nate's boat suddenly began to turn away from the yacht. Greta threw up her arms as if to say sorry.

No! That was my one chance to escape. The thought of being trapped for the entire night made my head spin. How could I possibly stay on the boat with Leo? I had to get off.

"I'm going to jump," I said, determined as ever. It was the perfect solution.

Jessie looked at me, speechless.

"Help me up... hurry... here, take my purse, and my shoes..." I breathed, as I peeled off the straps of my heels and began to climb up onto the side railing. Jessie grabbed the shoes and held out her hand to help steady me as I hoisted myself up.

At the thought of submerging myself in the bay, I paused for a brief second on top of the railing, the green silk of my dress clinging to me in the breeze. All of a sudden, the image from *Roman Holiday* flashed in my head: Audrey perched at the edge of the dock with all of her clothes on. She had jumped. I took a deep breath and stared at the dark water. When I put on the dress, I had no idea just how Audrey-like I would be that night.

"*Dove*?" Leo's voice bellowed out from behind me. "What the hell are you *doing*?"

There was no more time to hesitate. Nate's boat had almost finished its turn now, and Leo's footsteps thudded behind me. Without looking back, I leapt forward.

Suspended in midair momentarily, I heard Leo shout my name once more before I hit the water feet first. Cold wetness surrounded me, and I came up for air to the sound of even more shouting.

"Dove!" Leo called out again, his voice wild with shock.

The sound of the splash and the screams from the yacht were enough to alert Greta. "Hold on! We're coming!" she cried out as Nate steered the little boat back in my direction.

The crazed shouts of Leo and others echoed off the water as lights flashed from the deck of the harbor cruiser behind me. I kicked and pulled my arms through the cold water, gliding quickly along toward the Duffy, suddenly grasping the fact that my picture was no doubt being posted in real time. I hadn't weighed the possibility of being the drama and gossip story of the night, but it was too late now.

Suddenly, the roaring sound of another boat's engine blasted from somewhere over my shoulder. "Clive!" Leo's voice shouted out from the side of the cruiser.

I turned my head and saw the Boston Whaler curve its way around the front of the yacht. The horn from the huge cruiser blared again, this time longer and louder.

Now only a few feet away from the Duffy, I kicked harder and reached out to grab the side of the little boat. Greta leaned over to grip my arm, and Nate stepped away from the wheel to help heave me in. Dripping wet, I laid back on the cushioned bench to catch my breath. The boat rocked back and forth from all the commotion and then lurched forward as Nate put it into gear, pointing it away from the yacht once again.

Behind us, the screams and shouts escalated, and I looked up just in time to see Leo hit the water in the distance. *Unbelievable.* He kicked through the water, swimming straight toward Clive's boat.

"Go! Go!" I cried to Nate as I bolted upright. Nate turned the wheel harder while throwing it into its fastest gear. The little boat puttered through the bay, farther and farther away from the yelling and shouting off the decks of the cruiser.

Nate looked over at me, frowning with confusion. "Where to?"

"Thanks, Nate. Bay Shores, across from Lido Island... that way." I pointed off to the right, and then looked behind me again. In the distance, Isaiah and Clive reached over the side to haul Leo onto the Boston Whaler.

"He's going to try to catch us! We have to hurry!" I said, moving over beside Greta.

The cold night air bit through my soaked dress, and I shivered, my wet hair clinging to my face and shoulders. The whaler's engine rumbled in the distance again as the boat began to turn in our direction.

Nate maneuvered around a group of moored boats, shortcutting through the middle of the harbor. The whaler buzzed behind us in the distance. "His boat is way faster! We can't outrun him. We'll just have to hope we have enough of a lead!" he shouted as the little boat reached the tip of Lido Island.

"Around that way... over there!" I pointed over to the left now as Nate's boat rounded the end of the island. I looked behind us again. Leo stood at the wheel of the whaler, which was speeding toward us, kicking back water in its wake and looking bigger and even closer now. Nate was right—the little electric boat was no match for it.

Up ahead, I could see the square, cape-cod windows of my house in the distance as Nate cut diagonally across the bay, but Clive's boat continued to gain on us, closing in. The tension and coldness gripping me, I willed the little boat along. "Almost there!" I said. "Three docks more. It's the gray one with the white railing!"

The roaring sound of the whaler blasted beside us just as Nate edged the Duffy next to the nearest side of the dock. Perched and ready, I cleared the one-foot gap, hopping barefooted onto the wooden boards.

Wheeling around, Leo pulled the whaler up close on the opposite side. Clive grabbed the wheel and Leo jumped onto the other edge of the dock.

"What the hell are you doing, Dove?" He stood panting with his soaked clothes hanging from his body.

"What the hell are *you* doing?" I answered. All the anger and sadness from the past ten weeks, then the past ten months, bubbled up inside. My heart pounded against my ribcage as I stood facing him, dripping wet.

The two boats' engines idled next to the dock. Everyone aboard waited, staring.

Leo shook his head at me. "What are you talking about?"

"I can't believe I almost decided to trust you again." The tears finally came now, and a sob emerged as my

229

despair reached the surface. "I. Hate. You." Despite the meaning of the words that dropped out of my mouth, my inflection was the opposite. The soft breathiness had sounded more like *I love you*.

"Dove, what happened? Tell me what's wrong," he pleaded.

He stepped out toward me, and I backed away. "I know everything, Leo."

He stared back at me, his eyes wide.

"I know about Clarissa." I raised my eyebrows at him, hating the sound of her name. "At what point were you going to tell me that she's pregnant? Before or after I moved to San Francisco?"

His expression fell when my words hit him. I waited for him to defend himself, to argue, or plead. Something... anything. But he just stood frozen as the color in his face slowly drained.

Standing there, watching his blank and shocked expression, it hit me. He didn't know. Clarissa hadn't told him. My head reeled. I had just assumed that Clarissa would have run to him first, thrilled to hook him to her forever.

Leo moved his gaze to his feet, and I stared back in silence. A breeze picked up across the water, sending another chill rushing through me. The stillness was broken only by the sound of water lapping against the sides of the dock. I hesitated, and then let the words come out. "You didn't know?"

He raised his eyes to meet mine. "No."

Again, silence fell over the dock as the two boats rolled in the water.

"I'm—I'm sorry, Dove." He turned, stepped onto Clive's boat and dropped into one of the seats.

Not knowing if I shivered from the cold or from the

shock of it all, I watched as the whaler's engine revved and the boat disappeared into the distance. *His best day.* Not anymore.

Chapter 33

"BUT DON'T YOU SEE, FATHER? EVERYTHING HAS CHANGED."
-SABRINA FAIRCHILD

Sabrina

Heat surrounded me as I twisted in the down covers. My eyelids fluttered as the darkness of night clashed with bizarre images and eerie flashes of Leo lingering like a strange vision in kaleidoscope colors. I turned my stare toward the brightness of the digital clock. 2:47. I'd climbed into bed only five hours ago. Slowly gaining my senses, I could now feel the dampness of my pajama top clinging to my chest, which was heaving. The horrific sensation of the dream gradually began to fade, only to fully give way to the burning feverishness. Thoughts of the chaotic night now emerged one after the other. I rolled over, my exhausted mind searching for blankness, and the heavy warmth forced me to sleep again.

BITS OF SUNLIGHT BEAMED through the gap in the

sheer curtains. I sat up in bed and tried to clear the fuzzy sensation in my head. The last two days I'd spent in and out of sleep had been a strange experience of hellish nightmares mixed with the frightening reality of what I only wished had been a bad dream. I gauged my own condition as I slipped out of bed. The fever had finally gone. I drifted over to the window seat, tucked my legs underneath me, and leaned my head against the cool pane of glass. The dock looked peaceful, floating out on the glassy water. It seemed two-faced almost, the way it sat there so cheerfully, the sunlight reflecting off its white railing, revealing nothing of the dark episode that had taken place just three nights before.

A light knock woke me from thought. The door opened, and my dad's head popped in. He eyed me carefully. "Hey... looks like you're finally feeling better. We've been worried," he said, easing onto the cushion beside me. "Hungry? Ready for one of my Sunday omelets?"

I shook my head and rested it on his shoulder. He answered my quiet with his own silence, and I closed my eyes. "Did you see what happened? On the dock?" I asked.

I felt his head nod. "We saw the boats outside our bedroom window—couldn't hear everything, but..." He paused. "So, have you been seeing him all this time?"

I opened my eyes, bracing myself for his disappointment. "We broke up in March. And now, well, you don't have to worry about it anymore because... it's over forever."

My frustration at my dad still lingered, mixing with the torturous idea of never being with Leo again. Never again. I grabbed my forehead, squeezing it with the palm of my hand as the idea gripped me deeper. I set my head against the window once more, letting the surge of tears come, not wanting to fight against them anymore.

My dad looked away, blinking at the floor. "I guess—I didn't handle the whole thing very well."

I rolled my forehead against the cold glass as I moved my gaze to his, taking in the half-apology. It was enough. I grabbed his hand and found a semblance of a smile. "Me neither."

AT DINNER, I DID my best to fake a laugh here and a smile there, but behind my forced pleasant mood lurked a hollow sadness that felt like it might never leave.

"So, what's up for you this summer, Griffy?" I asked, searching for some sort of conversation.

"I'm going to sleep-away camp!" he piped up, his mouth full of food.

"Really?" I raised my eyebrows at him. "Very cool."

My stepmom's silent glances at me were filled with uncertainty... sadness. Disappointment was probably mixed in there, too. I didn't know what to think of it since I felt sorry and not sorry all at the same time. Come to think of it, that was probably exactly how she felt, too. Awkward silence hovered in the room, interrupted only by the clink of a fork here and there.

I strung a few sentences together in my head, trying to weave through a mixture of thoughts, gearing myself up to make the announcement. I'd made the decision earlier that morning, and ever since that moment, something had settled inside me.

I drew in a long breath. Might as well dive in headfirst. "I've decided I'd like to go to Parsons this fall."

My dad and Patty stopped chewing simultaneously.

Griffin's eyebrows popped up. "Is that in Paris? Can I come visit you?"

"Absolutely." I winked at him.

He stood up from the table and asked to play Xbox, knowing in his infinite ten-year-old wisdom that this would be the perfect time to leave.

I sat back in my chair to meet my dad's wide eyes, and the details of why poured out half-eloquently and half-stilted. He faked a casual composure during the parts involving Leo, and the fact that he didn't barrage me with a bunch of questions somehow helped me to be more straightforward as I got closer to the point.

"I guess it's simple. I really want to focus on my art now. I know I can do that anywhere, but... well..." I eyed my dad, bracing for his reaction. "Parsons has given me a merit scholarship—for the first year at least."

My dad blinked at me and slowly finished his mouthful of food. He knew I'd been accepted, but I hadn't told him about the scholarship. He cleared his throat, but made no protest.

"Paris..." Patty shifted in her chair. "It just seems so drastic."

I shook my head at her doubtful look. "It's not that crazy of an idea, Patty. We all knew I was applying to Parsons, and I found a way to earn it. I'd like to go. At least for the year, just to see..."

Sabrina's words played back in my head: *Paris is for changing your outlook.*

All this time I had spent preoccupied with Audrey's loves, I had completely forgotten about another love. One that Audrey had never seemed to neglect—a love for herself, for her own dreams. Now that I remembered, I was determined not to let myself forget again so easily.

"I just don't want you to make any fast decisions,"

Patty winced, shaking her head. "This looks to me like you might be running away from everything."

I stared at her, swallowing my bite of dinner as I took in the sight of her long, blinking lashes. Had she always had this earnest side? Maybe I had been too quick to judge her and her closet filled with stretchy pink sport tops. It was a legitimate point, but I already knew the answer. In fact, I'd never been so sure of anything in my life.

I bit the inside of my cheek and then found a genuine smile for her. "I'm not running away from anything, Patty. I'm running toward my dream."

MY SUITCASES LAY OPEN and half-filled on the floor as I dug through my closet with clothing piled at my feet. Jessie sat on the bed with her legs crossed, looking perfectly at home in the middle of the huge mess. In her hand she held the tiny snow globe I had bought at the theater.

"How is your dad taking all of this?" she asked, shaking the snow into a flurry.

I moved over to my dresser and opened the top drawer, searching around inside. "I think he's worried, but he said he supports my decision. He was pretty good about it when I told him everything."

"Everything?" Jessie's eyes went wide. "You told him about Santa Barbara?"

I glanced up. "Oh, well—no, not about Santa Barbara, but... I'm going to tell him."

"When?"

I looked down into the drawer, continuing my search. "When I'm thirty."

Jessie burst out laughing as she lay back onto the bed. She shook the little globe again, swirling the white snow around the tiny theater inside. "Have you talked to Henry?"

"No—I don't really want to. Not now. Besides, he's busy working."

"I don't know why you don't just hang out with hot Henry all summer," Jessie said as I shut the top drawer and opened the middle one. "What are you looking for?"

"My favorite blue sweater," I said, closing the drawer. "Hot Henry is touring the country with his theater group."

"Exactly. You could follow him around—be his groupie."

"I don't think so, Jess. Maybe you should," I added, raising my eyebrows at her.

She chuckled. "Nah. Isaiah and I are back together."

I spun around. "Really?" I said, my mouth falling open. "What? When did this happen?"

"Right after the whole thing went down on the dock with Leo." She dipped her head sideways. "He called me and said he missed me."

"I knew it." I narrowed my eyes at her, grinning.

"Yeah…" She shrugged. "I guess seeing you guys go through all that made him rethink everything."

The grin on my face grew even bigger. It finally happened. And I didn't feel half as bad about leaving now. As the days had crept by, signing up for two summer courses at Parsons had seemed more and more like the right decision. Dragging out the moving process over the entire summer would have only made everything more painful.

Opening the bottom drawer, I dug around for a moment before pulling out my blue sweater. As I started to close the drawer, I stopped. Inside, the colorful corner of a drawing peeked out from underneath a stack of T-shirts and I grabbed it, sliding the paper out slowly. The words *LEO and DOVE* floated above our smiling faces. I let the surge of pain sweep through me before I slipped the picture back into the drawer, folding my sweater on top of it. On second thought, the blue sweater didn't need to go to Paris.

Jessie watched me, propped on her elbow, her head resting on her hand. "I've got to admit, though—deep down, I thought you guys were meant to be."

I hopped up and headed back over to the cluttered closet.

Jessie paused before she spoke again. "Kai showed me a picture of them the other day."

At the word *them*, I flinched without warning. How could Leo and Clarissa be *them*? I took a summery dress off its hanger, not turning to meet Jessie's gaze. "Really?"

"Clarissa posted a photo of them out to lunch together. She's really got her claws into him now."

I didn't answer.

"Are you okay?"

"Yes." I folded the dress and put it into the larger suitcase.

Jessie sat up. "Wasn't sure if I should tell you."

"Of course you should tell me." I made my voice as casual as possible, willing myself not to picture them sitting together side by side, eating... talking.

A heavy quiet settled over us, and I knew Jessie was studying me. She sniffed before she spoke. "I can't believe you're really going through with this."

I broke my trance-like stare at my suitcase and looked up at her.

"We're..." She hesitated. "We're not going to get our one last summer together."

My own tears welled at the quiver in her voice, and I jumped onto the bed, tackling her with a hug. "I'm gonna miss you, too, Jess." A few stifled sobs kept her from answering. "Maybe you can come visit me, and we'll rock Europe together. Plus, I'm not going to miss coming to Boston to see you."

"Okay," she sniffed again, nodding.

"C'mon." I sat up. "We've made it all the way from first grade. Nothing can change our friendship now."

"Yeah," she said, sniffing the tears away again. "Wait." She sat up all of a sudden with a serious look. "Wait—there actually is something important I need to ask you."

I searched her face, slowing down. "Okay."

She raised her eyebrows, blinking with seriousness. "This summer, since you'll be gone... can I drive your convertible?"

We fell back onto the soft pillows, laughing, and I tried not to imagine what life would be like without Jessie.

Chapter 34

Roman Holiday

I stood in the doorway of my bedroom and paused, staring at Audrey's poster. One last time, I reached up to her smiling face and pressed my hand against the glossy paper before I flipped off the light.

Outside, my dad was waiting with the car engine idling. I hugged Patty and Griffin before I slid into the seat next to my dad, shutting the passenger door. Griffin held Patty's hand as he stood waving in the driveway, making every effort not to cry, his smile fading just a little with each rush of tears. This was it.

The car pulled onto the street, and I watched out the window as the houses fell behind, one after the other. As we crossed the bay bridge, I stared out at the harbor and drank in one last look, burning it like a postcard into my mind. Over my other shoulder, the cliffs towered over the Back Bay. At the top of those cliffs was the baseball diamond. I couldn't see it, but I didn't need to—the image of Leo on the field was clear in my memory. My mind wandered more. Where would he be right now? Headed to dinner somewhere with Clarissa by his side?

"Well." My dad broke the silence. "First place you sightsee? What's it going to be?"

"The Seine," I said without hesitating.

"The Seine?" He looked puzzled.

"Seriously, Dad? It's the river that runs through the city."

All my life I'd lived near the ocean and the bay, connecting to the water like some kind of silent muse, always fueling me to paint or draw. Right away, I wanted to see this famous river that I hoped might become a new source of inspiration for me.

"Oh right," he said, shrugging. "Thought you were going to say the Eiffel Tower or something."

"Yeah. Well, that, too." I looked out the window again.

"Food's supposed to be great," he said, making another effort at small talk.

"Mmhmm."

"But, you know, their omelets aren't going to be better than mine. I don't care if it is a French dish."

I couldn't help but laugh. His attempt at staying lighthearted made me miss him already. It was obvious he was suffering more than a little. And I would know. I was skillfully learning to ignore the constant ache I felt for Leo. Every day it lingered under the surface, threatening to spring up at any moment.

When we pulled to a slow stop next to the curb in front of the airport terminal, my dad reached out to grab my hand. "I just wanted to say..." he hesitated, "Mom would be really proud of you." He cleared his throat but didn't say another word.

Mom would be proud. I breathed it in. Yes... she would. "Thanks, Dad. That... means a lot." I squeezed his hand, and for a few seconds I matched his silence before reaching out to open the car door. Noisy airport sounds echoed all around as I stepped out onto the white curb.

He unloaded the bags from the trunk and set them beside me. "You're sure you don't want me to park and come in with you?"

"I'm sure." I raised my eyebrows and shot him a this-is-it grin. "I really love you."

He reached out, wrapping me in a hug. "Love you, baby," he said, his squeeze lasting much longer than normal. "Call us when you get there."

I wheeled the two suitcases behind me, turning my head to send him one last smile as he pulled the car from the curb and drove away.

Clasping onto my shoulder bag, I checked my luggage and then headed through the huge corridor toward the security gate. In the distance, along the far wall hung a series of large, framed paintings of marina settings and seascapes. I studied them from far off, but as I came closer, the details of one particular sailboat came crisper into view and caught my interest as I neared the escalator. The artist had captured it perfectly; the boat seemed to almost bob on the open sea. People rushed past on their way up the escalator, their heads obstructing my view of the painting here and there.

But one of the heads did not move. At the bottom of the escalator in front of the sailboat painting, one person stood still. A zinging energy pulsed through me.

Leo.

With his hands shoved into his pockets he stood transfixed on me, his dark, long-sleeved T-shirt clinging to his shoulders and chest.

I came to a stop in front of him, not moving my eyes from his. The familiar want crept up from inside. Some things were timeless, mindless, beyond understanding. My love for Leo was one of them. Denying it was useless.

His eyes flicked down and up, examining my expression. "Hi."

I blinked away my surprise. "Hi."

"Aren't you going to ask me what I'm doing here?"

Too many questions had gone without answers. I had nothing left inside to try to make sense of it anymore. "No, I'm not."

"Okay." He glanced at the floor. "Well, uh, I just wanted—I really need to..."

I studied him as his voice trailed off. "Say goodbye?"

He shook his head at me. "No." He frowned and shook his head again. "No. I just—I found out something today that you need to know."

I searched his face again. He was holding back tears, but a bit of emotion seeped out, twisting his expression.

"What is it, Leo? Are you okay?"

He let out a gushing breath and looked up, grabbing the back of his neck. Still staring at the ceiling, he nodded. "Yes, that's what I'm trying to tell you." He reached out, catching my hands into his. "My mom insisted on a paternity test. The baby's not mine."

My breath caught as I grabbed him and pulled him to me, holding on tightly, burying my head into his neck. His skin was warm against my face and I reveled in it, not believing I was actually touching him again. Loud intercom announcements boomed into the terminal while, all around, people filed past us onto the escalator.

He pressed his mouth to my ear. "Please don't go, Dove," he whispered. "Stay. Come to San Francisco. I

243

don't want to be without you."

The words fell into me like beautiful answers to my sadness as I felt his heart beat against mine. Pieces of my life began to whirl in my head like moving images. Painting on the dock, my mom sick in the hospital, Jessie's laugh, Leo coming down the hallway, the kiss at the fair, the fence at Clive's house, stepping off the train, rolling in the sand, Griffin's sweet face, Henry on the stage, Clarissa at the top of the stairs. The flashes kept coming, doing battle with one another, over which held more importance, more sway.

My mind continued to swirl with confusion and fuzzy memories of Audrey endings. Stay together. Or be torn apart. *Sabrina* or *Roman Holiday? Roman Holiday* or *Breakfast at Tiffany's*? It seemed like now the choice was torturous, yet simple… a heartbreaking goodbye, or a ride off into the sunset together.

I closed my eyes, trying to clear my head. None of that mattered anymore. The only thing that mattered was what *I* needed, what *I* would decide. I pressed my head into his chest, feeling it rise and fall with each breath, and then looked up at him. His dark eyes silently communicated—begging me and wanting me and loving me.

It was nearly impossible to say it. "I'm going to Paris, Leo."

Anguish sprang into his face, and he shook his head at me. "Why?"

"Because I need to—and I want to."

He didn't move, his face frozen in shock.

I glanced at the floor and back to his desperate eyes. "I'm so sorry."

He reeled. "I *love* you, Dove." His voice was almost a whisper, but the torment in it screamed at me.

Every bit of me steeled itself against crumbling. My head spun, searching for words to tell him what was inside of me, to somehow make him understand. "Maybe... maybe we had the right love, Leo. But just—at the wrong time." The last word caught in my throat as the tears finally surged and tumbled out. Maybe if we had met in the future, things might have been different. But too much had happened, and too much still dangled unanswered in whatever was ahead.

Still, it *was* the right kind of love. Despite everything, we'd really had that. The sweetest kind. The kind you find in fairy tales and Shakespeare plays and Audrey Hepburn films. Nothing could ever take that away.

It was what I held onto when I took a step back from him, shifting the bag on my shoulder.

Time to go.

He didn't move his eyes from mine as the escalator whisked me upward, floating me higher and higher as I watched him stand there, becoming smaller with each second that passed.

At the top, I tore my eyes from his, turned, and stepped out. Up ahead, towering windows stood at the end of the long hallway in front of me, framing the orange and purple shades of the sunset. I took a deep breath, lifted my chin, and walked toward it.

About the Author

Happy LaShelle is a writer, mom of three, and wife to a Basque baker who brings home loaves of crusty sourdough everyday. She lives near the mission bells in sunny Santa Barbara, but she loves the rainy banks of London's Thames River just as much as the sandy shores of her Newport Beach hometown. She studied History at UCLA and has a passion for Shakespeare plays, period films, and iced mocha lattes. ACCORDING TO AUDREY is her debut novel.

Acknowledgements

First and foremost, I want to thank my agent, Faye Atchison, who loved this manuscript from the very beginning and guided me along the path to making it the book it is today. I am forever grateful.

Thank you to the magnificent, super-powered team at CTP: Rebecca Gober, Courtney Knight, Melanie Newton, Marya Heidel for the gorgeous cover, and everyone working so hard behind the scenes. All of you inspire me with your passion and drive to create great books, and I'm honored to work with you.

Susan Dennard, you are my writing mentor—and you are the best kind: giving, patient, knowledgeable, smart, and so talented. Thank you for your selfless generosity and unending support on this journey to publication.

John Shepherd, thank you for beta reading and for loving my book. Your insight and genuine enthusiasm helped me to get up, dust myself off, and revise one more time. Joanna Hyatt, thank you for your encouragement and friendship on this author path, and for getting me my first writing gig! Big thanks also to Marissa Freeman and Sean P. Brady: Your detailed, thoughtful perspectives on the manuscript helped to steer me in the right direction.

To my mama, whose idea of a fun afternoon was to visit the used bookstore, the library, or the children's bookstore around the corner. You instilled in me a love for books that wrapped around my heart and never let go.

To my dad and my brother: You guys are two of the kindest, most generous men I know. Thank you for your love, and thanks for letting me hang out with the boys and learn about baseball.

Gerri, your genuine love is the truest and dearest, and a light in my life. Thank you for loving our family fiercely and for being my biggest fan.

To Hadley, Jack, and Grace: Your three beautiful souls bring mine so much joy. You are everything to me and I'm blessed to be your mom. Thank you for the many, many cuddles, and for your sweet support of my writing.

John, I'm beyond grateful for you, my incredible husband. Your enthusiastic encouragement, unwavering love, and crazy sense of humor keep me going. I adore you. Thank you for believing in me and never stopping!

Most of all, thank you to Patricia, for helping me to rediscover my calling, for being the best fairy godmother, and for cheering me along the entire way.